Maïa
of Thebes
1463 B.C.

THE LIFE AND TIMES

MAÏA
OF THEBES

1463 B.C.

BY ANN TURNER

Scholastic Inc.   New York

This book is dedicated to my wonderful writers' group who listened to all the many versions and kept me on a true course.

Copyright © 2005 by Ann Turner

Library of Congress Cataloging-in-Publication Data

Turner, Ann Warren.
Maïa of Thebes : 1463 B.C. / by Ann Turner. — 1st ed.
p. cm. — (Life and times series)
Summary: A young Egyptian girl, whose brother secretly taught her to read and write, accuses her uncle of stealing grain from the temple and must run away from Thebes to survive.
ISBN 0-439-65223-5
1. Egypt — Civilization — To 332 B.C. — Juvenile fiction. 2. Thebes (Egypt : Extinct city) — Juvenile fiction. [1. Egypt — Civilization — To 332 B.C. — Fiction. 2. Thebes (Egypt : Extinct city) — Fiction. 3.Uncles — Fiction. 4. Brothers and sisters — Fiction.] I. Title. II. Series: Life and times (Scholastic)

PZ7.T8535Mai 2005   [Fic] — dc22   2004022386

10   9   8   7   6   5   4   3   2   1   05 06 07 08 09

The display type was set in Sophia. The text type was set in Mrs. Eaves.
Book design by Elizabeth B. Parisi

Printed in the U.S.A.
First edition, April 2005

PROLOGUE

"Teach me." She grabbed Seti's wrist. "Teach me, I beg of you."

"But, Maïa, girls do not become scribes — they do not learn to write."

"I heard of one, Brother, who did so. You know that a scribe's life is an easy one — clean hands, barley beer with your meals, respect from others."

Respect. That was it. Not the beer or the good food or the clean hands. They did not matter to her, but to be looked up to, to be valued. She wanted it the way a starving child snatches at a piece of bread.

Seti let out a sigh.

"Remember our mother and father. Our father knew some signs and would have taught me had he lived."

"Had he lived." Her brother sighed again. The wind rustled the dry leaves in the shade tree above.

"And look at Her Majesty, Hatshepsut. She is a woman and

our ruler. The expedition has just come back from Punt with incense trees, gold, baboons, and all manner of exotic things. She has power."

Seti did not sigh this time, but in the dusk Maïa could see him nodding.

"Remember, I am your only sister, and you, my only brother. If you do not help me, who will?"

"All right. I will teach you, Maïa, but no one must know. No one!"

CHAPTER ONE

"Maïa? Ma — ï — ï — aa!" Aunt's voice was high and thin. "Where are you, girl?"

Maïa shrugged her shoulders impatiently as she stood on the flat roof of their mud-brick house, looking out. The heat rose from the land below, striking her head, face, and arms. The gold rays of the setting sun lay across her raised hands.

Over to her left, the river wound through the green land. At the edge of the green was the red desert — *deshret* — a place of robbers and demons. It was the Nile that gave them life — fish, and papyrus to make the paper that her brother wrote on in The House of Life, where he studied to be a scribe. The river gave life and it took it away, for hadn't her mother and father fallen ill after a night in Father's boat on the water?

Aunt had whispered the word "demons" and said a prayer to Bes, the household god, to guard them from evil. Perhaps it *was* a demon that caused her parents' death. All she knew was this: Mother and Father had burned and shriveled with heat until their breath had flown away, leaving Seti and her orphans. Then Maïa and her brother had landed on the hard shores of their aunt's house — Aunt Nebet.

"Girl, Ipi needs your help for supper! Did we not give you a home and you repay our kindness so?" The word "kind-ness" was two shrill, drawn-out syllables.

It was a familiar lament from Aunt Nebet — how much she had done for her and Seti, and how badly Maïa had repaid her. Maïa shrugged her shoulders again, reluctant to descend the stairs and see the angry face of her aunt.

What was that, over to her left, swaying in the tall reeds by the flooding river? Perhaps someone had been out fishing and was bringing his boat in. Yet there was something furtive about it, and though she watched, no one appeared to drag the boat up on the bank.

"Maïa! You had better come this instant!"

Turning, she saw the nearby cooking fires glowing red in the courtyards of other houses. Quickly, she ran down the outside stairs that led from the roof to the ground. A slight figure bent over the cooking fire, stirring something in a clay pot.

Ipi, their servant, straightened as Maïa came up to her. "Where have you been?" she whispered. "The mistress is so angry she spits!"

What did it matter what she did? Maïa imagined that when Aunt was born, she fought her way out of her mother's body, bawling and scowling. Perhaps she shook one tiny fist to show her displeasure at being born.

Maïa laughed but had to cover her mouth when Aunt Nebet swept into the courtyard.

"There you are, you ungrateful niece!" The braids in her hair were so tight they looked as if they hurt. She grabbed Maïa's wrist. "You have seen the river rise and fall thirteen times, old enough to help and be married. Though who would want a girl who is never here when wanted. . . ." She stalked off without a backward glance.

Maïa knelt by the fire, poking at it with a stick. She would poke Aunt's braids — so! — she would poke her back — so!

"Words, Maïa, they are just words. Go cut up some cucumbers and put out a plate of dates. Your uncle is very fond of them, as you know."

They giggled together, knowing that if a dish were put near Uncle Hay, the dates would disappear in a moment, an *at.* When Maïa returned from the back room, Ipi threw a handful of rosemary into the cooked lentils and lifted the pot off the fire.

They both arranged plates on the table in the main room, and Ipi stood on tiptoe to pull up the window shade. A small breeze made its way into the room.

"Where is your uncle?" Aunt stood in the doorway, twisting her copper bracelet. "He is never late for supper."

Seti appeared in the courtyard, coming home from working at his lessons at the temple. Though a year younger than Maïa, he was as tall as she, with a narrow face and intelligent eyes. He greeted her with a warm smile and went off to splash his face and hands with water before eating.

Finally, when they were all seated by the table, Uncle hurried into the room, white kilt flapping about his thin legs. They looked wet, to Maïa, and a faint trace of mud was on his ankles, above his sandals. He, too, went to wash, and returned without his wig.

"It is too hot for my wig, and now that I am not in the temple, I need not wear it. What are you looking at, Niece?" he said sharply, sitting on his stool.

"Nothing, Uncle." His brown, shaved head perched on his neck like an afterthought, and his long, thin legs seemed more like a spider's than a human being's.

"Did you help your aunt this day, Niece?" He tore his bread into tiny pieces. He put one in his mouth at a time, chewing with his mouth open.

"Yes, Uncle. Ipi and I made bread — as you can see." She ducked her head, then saw Seti touching the small crescent scar on his right shoulder. It was their warning signal: *Be careful. Keep your mouth shut.*

Uncle dipped his fingers into the bowl of water, then scooped lentils into his mouth. Yet he stopped midbite, some of the lentils falling back onto the table. Aunt sent him a worried glance and poured out the barley beer.

Maïa wondered what was wrong: Uncle *never* stopped eating midbite. And as a priest who was always fastidious, he never let food fall from his mouth. Maïa's arms prickled, and the hair on the back of her neck rose. This happened sometimes — a sense of what was to come. It felt like a thunderstorm rolling over the Nile; it felt as if, somehow, the god Seth were at hand, bringing evil and chaos.

Maïa began to chatter, "Brother, what did you learn today?"

He set down his bread. "I am memorizing all the signs for the gods and goddesses, the royals, marks of trade, and numbers. I now know over two hundred signs, enough to begin writing with, and am beginning the flowing script."

Maïa had trouble catching her breath. He was getting ahead of her! How could she catch up? How could she ever fulfill her dream of becoming a scribe when she — a girl — could not go to school?

Uncle smiled and tapped his fingers on the table. "I did well to put you in The House of Life to learn how to write and count. You can work at the temple and need never soil your hands."

Unlike me! Maïa sucked in a breath, choking on a lentil. Aunt Nebet pounded her hard on the back, and the lentil popped into Uncle's lap.

"What are you doing? These are my temple garments!" He stood, brushing angrily at his white linen kilt. "You know the Opet Ceremony is coming, and I must be ready, with clean clothes and a purified mouth."

"Yes, Uncle."

"And useless girls throwing lentils about will not help me at all!"

"No, Uncle."

Wiping his mouth, he headed toward the door. "I cannot eat any more, Wife. . . ."

"But, Husband, this is so unlike you. Did you have a bad dream last night?"

"No, Wife — I am nervous about all our preparations. All must be perfect for our . . . Her Majesty."

Maïa thought he did not show the proper reverence when he said the word "Majesty."

"Wearing king's garments, the *shendyt* kilt — the *nemes* headcloth . . ." he muttered, pacing the room. "Ruling like a man . . . It is not right, it is not according to Maat," he said, speaking of justice and rightness in the world. He strode outside, leaving the three of them gaping after him.

"Well, that is most odd," Aunt said, rising from her low stool. "My husband is not himself today."

"But why is he so angry at Hatshepsut?" Maïa said when she and Seti were alone. "Mistress Hunro says she is a good ruler, a peace-bringer to Egypt."

"That may be so." Seti patted her arm comfortably.

"But some hate the idea of a woman ruler and think it is time for her nephew, Tuthmosis, to be king." He paused. "Maïa, be careful and stay out of Uncle's sight. He is like a cat on hot earth."

Maïa sighed. She did not know how to be careful, but she thought she could stay away from Uncle, at least until the Opet Ceremony was over. Quickly, knowing that if she appeared busy Aunt would not chastise her, Maïa went to help Ipi clean up as the sky darkened, rubbing the small clay dishes with stiff reeds and rinsing them with water. They hung the leftover bread in a net bag against the wall of the back room, away from mice.

"Maïa!" her brother called from the rooftop. "Come up and be with me."

After she had climbed the stairs to the roof, Seti patted his sleeping mat, inviting her to unroll hers and lie down. "Tell me a story about the old days, in Father's house."

"And Mother's." In a low voice, she described Father setting out in his reed fishing boat with Mother beside him, hair blowing back in the breeze, and Miw, their cat, sitting in the prow of the boat.

Maïa closed her eyes, shutting out the glittering white stars above. Inside she saw the waters of the

Nile rocking the boat, rocking her parents who were gone forever. Maïa curled her arms around her body, holding her sorrow inside. Somehow she had to find a way out of this house, away from unkind looks and sharp words. But how?

CHAPTER TWO

Dawn came suddenly. Maïa sat up and looked at the sky. The star they called Sopdet, which signaled the start of the Nile's flooding, twinkled low in the sky. Red lay on the horizon, and she heard cries of morning birds and the sounds of people waking on the rooftops of houses nearby. A dog barked, settled, then a baby cried.

She looked over at Uncle still asleep on his mat, his mouth slightly open. Aunt slept all curled up, like a child, her arms tucked beneath her legs. To foil demons?

But Seti was awake — as always. They crept down the stairs to the courtyard before anyone else was up. The air had a fresh, clean smell, not filled with the dust and heat of later on.

Seti lifted his scribe's kit off his shoulder and handed it to Maïa. Quickly, she took the small flask and ran to fill it from the reflecting pool. As she set it down, Seti grinned at her, dipped his reed brush into the water, and stroked it across the black ink in his palette, which had two hard circles — one for black ink and one for red.

"Red is only for emphasis, right, Brother?" Maïa crouched beside him.

"That's right — to put a line under an important hieroglyph or for the signs of gods and goddesses. Also, unlucky days, remember?"

Maïa shivered. She hoped that today would be a lucky day. "Seti, you are getting ahead of me. I do not have the time you have." She struck one hand on the ground. "I need to learn!"

"We will go as fast as we can. Do not be discouraged. You are far smarter than many of the other boys in my class and do not need to be beaten like some."

In the faint gray light Maïa smiled, and she saw her brother's answering smile — a slash of white in his face. "You know over one hundred signs already. Today I'll teach you Hatshepsut's name." He pulled a piece of broken pottery toward him.

First, he made two oval cartouches to contain the names of their ruler, then wrote the signs of the reed and the bee in one, symbolizing her rule over Upper and Lower Egypt. As he wrote, Maïa made the signs with a stick in the dirt. But before they could finish, Maïa sensed someone nearby.

"Ipi!"

"What are the two of you doing?"

Maïa stood, brushing her foot over the signs in the dirt, but Ipi was too quick and knelt beside Seti. "You are teaching her to write!" Her voice was almost accusing.

"I made him teach me — oh, do not tell Uncle, you know how he distrusts me!"

The girl rose. "And why would I do anything to hurt the two people who are kind to me in this house?" Even though she was older than Maïa, Ipi only came up to her shoulder, and she looked like a plant that had not been properly watered.

"I did not know that girls could be scribes," Ipi said, "but I will never tell your secret."

"But our ruler, Hatshepsut, must know how to write," Maïa said stubbornly. "Why should I not learn?"

The girl nodded and limped slightly as she went

over to start the morning cooking fire. They had an unbreakable bond where each admired the other's courage. It came from a time not long ago when they were washing clothes in the Nile.

Ipi was pounding the clothing with a stone when suddenly she cried out, and the water thrashed beside her. "Crocodile — my foot!" Ipi screamed.

Maïa whapped the clothing against the water, hoping to scare off the creature, but it did not help. Yelling, Ipi raised the stone and thumped it down on the crocodile's eye. The tail slapped the water, then disappeared.

"Hurry, hurry!" Maïa grabbed Ipi and helped her onto the riverbank. She made her sit, as an unearthly sound came out of the girl's mouth, "*Eeee, eeee!*"

Maïa ripped one of Uncle's kilts into strips, bound Ipi's bleeding foot, and wrapped an arm around her. Maïa helped Ipi limp home, where she laid her on the cool floor.

Aunt flapped her hands at Maïa, trying to shoo her outside, but Maïa would not move Ipi again. At the sight of all the blood, Aunt ran from the room, crying out, "A bad day, Niece, this is an unlucky day!"

Surprisingly, Uncle had known what to do. He

brought wine to wash the wound and told Maïa to bind it tightly with linen. Maïa was happy he did not realize it was his torn kilt that had been used for bandaging the girl's foot.

Amazed at Uncle's concern, Maïa later heard him talking with her aunt. "The wine will help such a wound to heal, Wife, and we shall be saved the trouble of searching for another servant. Ipi is not expensive to keep, for she eats so little."

Ever since then, Ipi was eager to serve both Seti and Maïa. Her foot eventually healed, but she still walked with a slight limp and was understandably reluctant to wash clothes in the Nile.

So Maïa knew she need not fear that Ipi would ever give their secret away. Quickly, she wiped away all traces of their writing lesson, then wrote what she remembered of Hatshepsut's name in the air — she must not forget! Learned in secret and practiced in the dawn, the hieroglyphs were hers.

Only a moment later she heard Uncle coughing, clearing his throat, and the sound of his feet slapping against the steps.

Aunt Nebet came rapidly after him, flapping her arms at her sides. "Husband, I dreamed that you were drinking warm beer, a sign for bad luck!"

Uncle Hay peered anxiously at her, holding out his amulet. "Why can you not dream of good luck, Wife? Such as a man with a bow in his hand."

Aunt lifted her amulet to the rising sun and murmured a prayer for protection. "Be careful this day, Husband. Watch the steps behind you. Guard the steps ahead of you. Choose the right path, not the wrong path. Stay in the shade."

The instructions rained down, and Uncle Hay grew paler and paler. After a time, he put his hands over his head and shouted, "Enough, enough! I will do what you say, Wife, just . . . stop . . . talking!" He staggered off to wash himself in the bathing room.

As they ate bread together and washed it down with barley beer, Uncle was still pale. ". . . Must remember — no fish and no beans before this sacred ceremony . . . There is so much to think about, Wife. . . ." He drummed his fingers on the table.

When he paused for breath, Aunt said, "I cannot wait to see Her Majesty. She will be at the temple of Luxor, Husband." It was not a question.

"Yes — you all can see her." He rose so quickly that his stool turned over.

"Husband, there is no need to hurry."

"But, Wife, all must be ready. Her Majesty is coming with all of her retainers and scribes who will look into . . ." He paused. ". . . Into . . ." His voice ran down, and he left them — once again — gaping at his surprising behavior.

"Well, then," Aunt said briskly. "There is much to do — all the rugs to be beaten, Ipi, and beer to be made — Niece — start right now."

Seti gave Maïa a sympathetic glance before he left for school at the temple. Maïa imagined herself going with him, wearing a scribe's kilt, carrying a writing kit, and going to practice the signs for sounds and those representing words and ideas.

"Hurry, Maïa," Ipi whispered to her. "Be busy before your aunt sees you."

Maïa hurried to crush the grain for making beer, pretending that she was a scribe at the temple writing in vivid red ink.

CHAPTER THREE

The day began with Uncle shouting, "Where is my kilt, Wife?" He ran about the room, opening a clothing chest, clutching one kilt in his arms, throwing another onto the floor.

Seti stood in the far end of the courtyard, touching the crescent mark on his shoulder again. Maïa leaned against him, trying to stay out of Uncle's way.

"I am an important man who oversees the grain of the temple — I am a servant of the god and must look well cared for!"

Ipi handed him a kilt that he deemed of the proper whiteness and appearance, but unfortunately, Uncle looked through the door at Maïa, who was smiling.

"Away with you, you good-for-nothing niece! Why did my sister not have a useful child? You are useless!"

Useless. The word pricked at her.

"Why are you angering my husband on this day of all days? He speaks the truth when he calls you useless!" Aunt stood in the doorway, hands on her hips, frowning.

Maïa's chest felt squeezed and tight; she could not breathe in this house with this fog of ugly words. Ducking her head, she ran out to the dry road.

"Maïa!" Seti called after her, but she did not turn back. With each step that she took, dust puffed behind her. Her throat ached, and she could not tell if it was from tears or from the heat that was already rising from the road.

She ran through the lane near theirs, wanting to put Uncle far behind, and passed a familiar house where the weaver, Mistress Hunro, was beating rugs outside. The old woman had been kind to her and Seti when they first came to Aunt's house. "Maïa! Come visit and tell me the news!"

Maïa paused for a moment. "I cannot . . . I must get away from . . ."

The old woman nodded. "I know how it is,

Daughter. Here, let me get some bread from the house — you are too thin." She stumped inside and returned quickly.

Thanking her, Maïa tucked the bread into her sash and darted out of the end of the lane. She passed a thickset man pulling his donkey by a rope and shouting at it to hurry. *I am that donkey,* she thought, *Uncle is the owner, and his words are the rope.*

Maïa stopped in the middle of the road and sighed. Her brother had shown her the hieroglyph that came at the end of the signs for tiredness: a man kneeling on the ground, arms outstretched. She crouched down, miming the pose.

The sound of voices and laughter raised her up, and she kept walking. No one would see her crouched in the road, feeling sorry for herself. She would go to market and see what animals were for sale. Perhaps there would be baboons, monkeys, or other creatures. She wished she had a little monkey — *ky* — that would perch on her shoulder and chatter. It would be kind, and it would love her.

The houses were closer together as she neared the center of Thebes, a jumble of brown and mud-colored houses with flat roofs. Heat rose from the street, banging from house to house like a clashing cymbal. Maïa paused to wipe the sweat from her face. On her right was a line of washing hung between two houses. A woman sang, beating a reed rug by her doorway. Boys darted about on errands for their masters. At the end of one lane she saw the white lines of the southern temple sparkling in the sun, and across the river were the red cliffs with the highest peak sacred to the cobra-goddess, She Who Loves Silence. The sounds of the city swelled, like music played at a festival. Maïa stepped faster, almost dancing.

A barrel-chested man held up a skinny dog. "See how fine his legs are! He has speed and grace and is loyal!" He opened the dog's mouth so people could see the white, shining teeth and flicked the dog's ears to show how clean they were.

The dog growled, and the man shook him. "Yes, indeed, loyal as Her Majesty is to her subjects, as the Nile floods, as the sun rises again in the east."

"Buying a dog is not a religious act," said an elegant woman nearby, and Maïa laughed. The woman turned, giving her a hard stare, then smiled.

"I would not buy a dog that growled," Maïa said. "I would not trust him."

"Nor would I." The woman beckoned, and Maïa stepped closer. A sweet perfume came from the woman's braided hair, and her eyes were outlined with gray on top and green malachite on the bottom. She wore a finely pleated linen shift, and a golden bracelet circled her upper arm. Clearly, she was a woman of means.

"What do you do here, girl?"

"I look at the animals, Mistress," Maïa answered. "I do like monkeys."

"I do not! Nasty, chattering creatures that make their messes everywhere." She shuddered. "Come here, Meret, my daughter." She crooked her finger at a girl in a fine linen dress, wearing gold jewelry, and about the same age as Maïa.

Meret was short, slight, with a pointed chin and the most astonishing dark eyes Maïa had ever seen. They were like a reflecting pool in the moonlight when the water gleamed and moved as if a god breathed on it. *I would make the sign, so. . . .* Unconsciously, Maïa made the sign for water at her side.

"What is that? What are you doing? Are you making evil signs? My daughter is a fine girl!"

Maïa sputtered and waved her hands. "Mistress, I did not mean to . . . I made no sign . . . I just moved my hand in the air." She flapped her hand up and down.

The woman's eyes narrowed. Coming closer, she tilted Maïa's chin in one hand. "No, that is not what you did. I saw, and you were not flapping your hand." She paused. "I should take you to a man who can undo spells. We cannot have people running about making evil signs on a sunny, fine day!"

Maïa felt as if she had been slapped. She stepped back one pace.

"Ah, Mother, why do you torture her? You can see she is innocent of any wrongdoing." Meret stepped forward and smiled for the first time. "I think that she is just someone's daughter, getting ready for the Opet Ceremony."

Maïa looked at her gratefully; her secret was safe for now, thanks to this girl.

Suddenly, there was a burst of sound off to their right. People screamed, men laughed, and a monkey swung onto a low roof. Chattering, he threw mud clumps on the people below.

One hit the elegant woman, and she shook her fist at the animal. "Son of a thief! Foul-mouthed, eye-running, stinking-breath baboon, begone!"

Meret's shoulders began to shake, then Maïa's, and soon they were doubled over, laughing together at the woman's outrage, which only infuriated the elegant woman. They did not see the monkey drop from the rooftop and scurry toward Meret.

Leaping onto her leg, the creature scrambled up her body, reaching for her gold jewelry. "*Aiee!* Get him off me!" Meret screamed, backing up and waving her arms. Her mother did not help, adding her screams to those of the girl.

Frightened by the noise and the crowd, the monkey bit Meret, and she yelled even louder. Maïa dashed forward and hit the monkey on his back, but he just clasped the girl's arm tighter, turning his face from side to side and chattering.

As Meret collapsed, her mother cried, "Will no one help us? Pashed, where are you?" Behind them, a tall servant cleared a space around Meret and pulled on the monkey's arm — to no avail.

Then Maïa took the piece of bread from her shift and held it out to the monkey, who bared his teeth and grabbed the bread. Stuffing it into his mouth, he jumped off Meret and scampered away.

"He bit me!" Meret cried, touching the rivulets of blood that streaked her skin.

The mother seemed frozen, unable to help, so Maïa crouched beside the girl, dabbing at the wound with her shift. "There, it will be all right, do not scream, it was only a silly *ky*."

Meret continued to sob, clutching her arm and groaning.

When the servant stepped forward and said, "Mistress, we should take the girl back to the inn and wash the bite," the woman seemed to come awake.

"Are you all right? Does it hurt?" She knelt beside her daughter, putting an arm around her. Meret only nodded, still crying.

The mother turned to Maïa and kissed her. "We are grateful to you! What would have happened if you had not gotten that beast away from my daughter!"

Maïa ducked her head, suddenly embarrassed. But she remembered her mother caring for an open cut on her leg long ago. "Mistress, after you wash the wound, put honey on it. My mother did so once when I was hurt."

The woman patted Maïa's shoulder. "You are a good girl. What is your name?"

"Maïa."

"And I am Nefert, and this is my daughter, Meret." Slowly, she rose, helping the girl to her feet. Supported by the servant on one side and her mother on the other, Meret began to walk slowly down the street.

"Come, come with us, Maïa," she cried.

Maïa followed, taking her hand. She soothed her, as if she were a child, not a girl about her age. "There, there," she said, singing songs of happiness.

Making their way through the crowd, they turned down a side street, went through a maze of other small alleys, and came at last to the Inn of the Ibis. Carefully, the party made their way up the staircase to Nefert's rooms.

Once inside, Nefert clapped her hands, and a servant girl appeared. "Bring me fresh water and, Pashed, fetch me honey from the innkeeper."

Maïa helped Meret lie down on a padded mat in the corner. When the servant girl reappeared with a flask of water, Maïa wet a cloth and cleansed the wound.

Pashed brought a small dish containing honey, which Nefert dipped her fingers into and dabbed on the bite. Together they ripped linen into strips and bound the wound.

"Thank you," Meret said. "It is better now."

"Say a prayer to chase away demons. She must

not fall ill, I have already lost one daughter!" Nefert commanded, lifting up her Hathor amulet.

Maïa held out her Bes amulet, praying for protection, health, and strength. When she was done, Meret sank back against the headrest, sighed, and fell asleep.

"You are a girl of courage and quick thinking." Nefert took Maïa to the corner of the room. "We are grateful to you."

"It was nothing, Mistress. Anyone would have helped. I think that monkey was just frightened by the noise and the crowd. Oh!" She clapped her hand to her mouth and ran to the door. "I must go, I am expected back home."

"Wait." Nefert stood with her on the top stair. "Where do you live? Who is your family?"

"My mother and father are dead, Mistress, but I live with my aunt and uncle on the outskirts of Thebes. My uncle Hay is a priest at the temple of Karnak."

Nefert's face suddenly closed in a grimace. What had she said wrong? Maïa wondered, but she must go, and she dashed downstairs and disappeared into the crowd, hoping to get home before Aunt's wrath fell on her.

CHAPTER FOUR

Maïa was dreaming her favorite dream. In it, she sat beside her mother on the roof of their old house. It was hot, as always, but a slight breeze blew in from the river. Father was out fishing, and Seti was asleep.

Mother sang to her of the goddess Hathor and how she cared for her human children and gave them the gifts of beauty and music. Her voice was soft as a flute and slid up and down on the notes. In the dream, Maïa held out a small clay jar. She fanned her hand downward, sending each sweet note into the jar, then sealed it with mud and a green reed tied around the mouth.

Somehow she knew that Mother had gone into the land of the west, leaving her and Seti alone. Her heart felt hollow and sore.

But remember my words, daughter mine. Remember the sweetness of my songs, and they will give you courage.

Still dreaming, Maïa realized that now she had to free Mother's songs from the clay jar. Frantically, she hit at the dried mud until pieces flew off in every direction. Holding her breath, she put her head down close to the opening.

One note rose — another followed — like leaves in a whirling wind, her mother's song flew into the air. When Maïa woke, her face was wet with tears.

Some sound had woken her. A dog barking? A donkey stamping hard on dry ground below? Sitting up, Maïa clasped her knees and looked around. All seemed as usual: the great sparkling sky — Nut — curved over the earth — Geb — with people sleeping on rooftops of houses nearby.

Aunt Nebet lay curled up like a small child. Even in sleep she frowned, and Maïa thought she was dreaming of some evil portent. Seti slept nearby, his arms flung out and face to the sky, unafraid.

But the fourth sleeping mat was empty. Perhaps Uncle Hay had had to use the chamber pot? He always complained about how barley beer made him get up at night. He was not to be seen — at the edge of the roof, going down the stairs, or returning.

She was tempted to lay back on the mat, to look up at the star Sopdet that signaled the rising of the Nile, and to think about the coming ceremony. She wondered if she could find her new friend, Meret, walking from the temple of Karnak down to Luxor.

Something thumped below, and Maïa heard a soft oath. Another thump, another curse. Was that the sound of their donkey stamping its feet?

Maïa crept to the edge of the roof and peered down. All she could see was the dim courtyard and a few embers from the cooking fire. She crept toward the back of the roof, where she could barely see the doorway that led to their underground storage room. In the flickering light of an oil lamp, a distorted shape with a huge hump for a back began to go down the steps.

She pressed her fist into her mouth — a demon? She held out her Bes amulet, muttering a prayer. "Let no evil befall us, Bes, guard us from demons and those who wish to take away our breath. . . ."

It did no good. Her heart thudded, and the figure reappeared at the top of the cellar stairs. It bent down, heaved something onto its back, and disappeared from sight again. No oaths this time, just the faint sound of heels on steps below.

An animal snorted, and the sound made Maïa draw back from the edge. She knew that sound; it was their donkey, Skinny One, and the figure below had to be Uncle. But what was he doing?

She waited for a moment, then saw the figure stop at the top of the stairs and blow out the oil lamp. He would be coming up to the roof, and she must not be seen! Maïa hurried back to her sleeping mat and pretended to close her eyes. For a while, nothing happened; Maïa's eyelids fluttered, and she pinched herself to keep awake. Suddenly, Uncle Hay was tiptoeing over to his sleeping mat and lying down.

She could not see his face but was certain he was smiling a small, satisfied smile. She could *feel* it in the dark under the star shine. And she was certain Uncle rubbed his right forefinger against the back of his left hand, always a sign that he was pleased. What in the name of Amun was Uncle up to?

In the darkness of early dawn, Seti followed her as she went quietly down the steps to the courtyard. "Get the water, Maïa, and I will find pottery shards to write on," he said. "You are almost as far along as I am. Father would have been proud."

Maïa sighed. "I cannot write with you today, Seti. There is something I must do."

"But you are coming along so well, Maïa, we must keep up!" Seti looked bewildered.

"I know, but remember what you said about Uncle being like a cat on scorched earth? I may know why, and it is best if I do this alone." Without explaining any further, she went around to the back of the house. She did not dare light a lamp.

Leaving the door open at the top of the stairs, she went down the cool steps into the small storage room. Hands out, she felt her way around, touching the jars of wine on the floor, a jar of barley, one containing oil, a small one with precious honey, and net sacks with spices, onions, and garlic.

Feeling her way, she went across the floor to the opposite wall, where she knew the other jars were stored. With one hand she felt the coolness of the clay surface and then — nothing. There was an open space where another jar should be.

She put her hand out again, praying there would be no spiders here. Then her hand touched the rough cloth of a sack. Feeling beside it, she found another sack, a third, a fourth, and a fifth. Pressing her hand against the cloth, she felt the grains inside rolling under her fingers. Were there any ties at the top? Often, a clay seal would tell where the wheat or barley had been grown.

But the seals had been torn off. Maïa paused; she was certain Uncle had stored the sacks here late last night. She was equally certain he did not want to be seen. A question formed inside, and Maïa remembered the hieroglyphs, one of the sentences Seti had taught her — *Shemek iref her see wat:* On what road are you going? She did not know the answer.

There was nothing to prove her suspicions. Frowning, she turned and started up the stairs. At the top, the light was stronger. Soon Ipi would be up, lighting the fire in the courtyard. Then Aunt would thump down the stairs from the roof, calling out instructions for the day. Uncle would come, too, clearing his throat in that way she hated and giving Maïa sharp, piercing looks.

Her bare feet stubbed on something on the top step — something hard and round. Maïa knelt and picked it up. It was a clay seal. There was not enough light yet to read it, but her fingers traced the signs:

I belong to the temple of Karnak.

CHAPTER FIVE

Maïa woke to the soft chiming of the sistrum, like wind in tall reeds. The instrument — shaped like a hollow rattle with a carved face of Hathor — was meant to calm the gods and goddesses and was always played at great festivals — such as — *today*!

Maïa's eyes flew open, and she stood immediately, realizing the chiming had been in her dreams. Aunt rose from her sleeping mat and stretched. Uncle was awake, too, all fidgets and darts and quick motions.

"Wife! Hurry, today is the day! I must be washed, and this is the last day to purify my mouth! Hurry!"

"Yes, Husband, no, Husband," Aunt grumbled,

but softly enough so that only Maïa heard. Maïa's head felt hollow and light, and she realized it was from lack of sleep. *Because of your uncle and his lies.*

She started; it sounded like someone speaking within, but it must just be her thoughts. The hard clay seal she'd hidden inside her shift dug into her skin — a reminder.

Aunt woke Seti, who sprang to his feet like a cat, calling out, "Maïa!"

"Yes, Brother, here I am." She rubbed her face and walked to the roof's edge. All looked as usual — the sparkling Nile overflowing its banks, with a farmer and his donkey plodding through the dry part of his fields.

The inside of her body churned like the swelling river, and she felt sick. *That is because the gods and goddesses hate lies. Your mother told you that.*

Pressing one hand to her mouth, Maïa ran down to the cooking fire where Ipi was preparing breakfast.

"Ipi?" she said to the bent figure. "Do I look well? Feel my cheeks — have I a fever?"

Ipi rose, looking harried, and put one hand on Maïa's cheek. "No, there is no fever. Are you ill?"

"I do not know, Ipi, it seems I am hearing . . ."

She stopped as Ipi bent, lifted the pot of cooked barley and dried grapes, and carried it into the main room.

"I hope you look better than that for the festival, Niece! My relatives must be well dressed and clean this day!" Uncle scooped barley into his mouth and coughed. "Nephew, keep your aunt and sister safe in the crowd."

Maïa smiled at her brother, happy that he was to be with them, but her smile faded immediately. She could not eat, sipping at her water as words rose up inside. *What will you do about your uncle?* the unbidden voice sounded inside. It must have been something she ate or not enough sleep. Grasping her Bes amulet in one hand, Maïa silently prayed for protection and asked rebelliously, *Why must it be me?*

Uncle looked strangely at her. She must have spoken the words out loud, and she began to gabble like a goose. "I am nervous about the festival. There is much to do!"

Because you saw it, the voice answered.

She started and turned over the flagon of water. Uncle jumped up before it could drip on him and strode out of the room, muttering.

"On this day of all days, girl! You are so clumsy.

Clean it up, for we have much to do before we can leave for the temple." Aunt strode out of the room.

"What is wrong, Maïa?" Seti rose and put his arm around her. "Now *you* are as fidgety as a cat on hot earth!"

"Because — because . . ." She put a hand over his, then closed her mouth. Nothing must interfere with his studies and his life at the temple. For a moment, Maïa leaned into his warmth. What would he think about inner voices telling her what to do? And Mistress Hunro — would she have any answers?

The gentle sound of a sistrum called Maïa outside; it reminded her of Mother. Sitting on the wall bench, Aunt shook her sistrum with her eyes closed. As wife of a priest, she would play it during the procession from the temple at Karnak to Luxor. For a moment, the muscle softened in Aunt's face.

Maybe if Maïa complimented her aunt, she would be kinder? "That was beautiful, Aunt Nebet."

"Thank you, Maïa," she said, giving her a rare smile. But when Aunt set down the instrument, her smile faded, and her voice rose to its usual commanding tone.

"Hurry! We must get ready right away. Ipi, Ipi, come to me at once!" she called out.

Ipi came into the courtyard holding Aunt's new wig, her cone of scented oil, and a tray of cosmetic pots. Setting them on the bench, she placed the wig on Aunt's head.

"There, you look lovely." Ipi fastened the perfumed unguent on top of the wig as Aunt fidgeted.

"Is it on right?" She felt it with one hand, then nodded at the servant. "My makeup."

Silently, Ipi held out a small pot. Aunt dipped a flat wooden stick into the gray pigment, spread it on her eyelids, and peered into her handheld mirror. "I wish we could afford a silver mirror!" she fretted, but Ipi reassured her that the color had gone on in the proper way.

"Maïa, do not stand there staring at me like a witless girl! Go bathe and put on the new dress I got for you. Your uncle has grain enough to trade for good things," she said in a satisfied voice, pulling on a copper armband and settling her red-and-blue-beaded necklace at the base of her throat. "Our neighbors must not think that a priest of the temple cannot properly dress his wife and niece!"

That priest of the temple who is stealing its grain.

Maïa pressed both hands to her ears as she went into the small room with a drain in the middle. Two bowls of water rested on the floor, with a reed brush for washing beside. Stripping off her old garment and hiding the clay seal beneath, Maïa poured water over her hair, arms, and body, and rubbed the soft brush and salt paste against her skin. But all the scrubbing and all the water could not wash away the sense of disaster crouching like a lion in the road ahead.

"Where is my new shift?" Maïa asked.

Aunt gave her a sharp glance. "Niece, we must fatten you up before we marry you. You are too thin. Men like their girls to have some curves."

Maïa did not even glance down; she knew her bones stuck out. Perhaps if Uncle were not so greedy, she could get more food at meal times.

Greed, that is the problem, is it not? Greedy like the crocodile.

"Child, what is wrong with you? You are like a bird pecking at the dust, flying this way and that."

Maïa thought rapidly. "I . . . um . . . do not wish to displease you."

Aunt told Ipi to bring the new shift from the clothes chest and the pair of reed sandals. When Ipi held out the clean garment, Maïa took it and buried her nose in the cloth. Clean — never worn by anyone else — hers.

"Thank you, Aunt, and thank Uncle for me."

Whirling around, she went back into the room, slipped her feet into the sandals, and pulled the dress over her head. She tied the cord around her chest and tucked the damning seal inside her shift. Somehow she would know what to do with it — maybe not now, but it would come to her.

"That is better." Aunt surveyed Maïa. "Come and I will put some makeup on your eyes."

Maïa tried to stay still while Aunt painted gray on her top lids and green beneath. For a moment she felt beautiful, with eyes like a lotus and fresh linen touching her legs. But the moment of calm disappeared, and Maïa felt her insides churn again.

Hatshepsut's retainers and servants would be at the temple; could they discover Uncle was stealing from them? How did they punish a thieving priest? And what would happen to Seti and her? The hieroglyph for thief — *ichu* — sprang up before her eyes, quickly followed by the sign for to die — *met*. Clearly, she saw the sign for a man falling with blood streaming from his head.

"Niece! Hold still! Stop fidgeting!"

Maïa forced herself to stand and not scrape her foot against her leg. Ipi gave her a sympathetic glance and pointed to her own clean dress.

Once Aunt was gone, Maïa dipped her finger into the green malachite, and rubbed some under Ipi's eyes.

"Maïa!" she breathed. "Your aunt?"

"Hush. She is playing the sistrum with other wives of the priests and will be too busy to see you. Come with us to the festival and be careful of stray dogs and strange men."

"You sound like the mistress." Ipi put the cosmetics away in the back room.

Aunt ran up and commanded, "Hurry, hurry! Maïa, is my cone fixed on properly?"

"You look lovely," Maïa said, but she choked as she heard, *All is not fine.*

Ipi took one look at Maïa's face and whispered, "Careful, Maïa. I, who bear the marks of a crocodile's teeth, sense danger. Please be careful."

CHAPTER SIX

Maïa's neck prickled from Ipi's words; they sounded like the start to an unlucky day. Could she be wrong? Maïa kept her eyes focused on her aunt, trying to think of cheerful things. She had to admit that Aunt looked magnificent — and unfamiliar, tall and regal, taking short, swift steps. The cone on her wig glistened in the hot sun. As the day grew warmer, the oil would melt and run onto her shoulders, showering her with fragrance — like the gods and goddesses. The sun shone on her copper armband, striking Maïa's eyes and making her flinch.

Seti and Ipi walked beside her, but even their company could not cheer Maïa. She felt as if there were a hollow space about her, filled with worries about Uncle's theft and the future.

"Stay near me, Niece. There are many strangers and foreigners at these festivals who would take advantage of a pretty girl like you. Seti? Guard your sister. Watch who walks beside you and behind you." Aunt paused to hand Maïa a light linen scarf.

Aunt walked surprisingly fast, and the other three hurried through the crowds of festival-goers dressed in their finery, heading toward the Karnak temple, just north of Thebes. Maïa was jostled by a crowd of women, eyes bright as flowers, singing all kinds of songs. Farther ahead was a man with a monkey on his shoulder.

She shivered, remembering the monkey biting her new friend. Would she be at the festival? Maïa hoped the honey had helped the wound to heal properly, and that Meret had no fever.

"Is something wrong?" Seti said in her ear. "You look worried."

Maïa looked at him, surprised he was still beside her. "No, nothing is wrong." *Except treachery.*

"Seti, Maïa, Ipi, hurry, don't get lost!" Aunt called.

Soon they reached the courtyard of the temple of Amun. Somewhere Uncle waited with the other priests, ready to make the joyful march down the avenue to the Luxor temple.

How can he walk in the procession? Maïa thought. *How can Uncle pretend to serve Amun when he is stealing his grain?* For a moment, she remembered Mother's words — that the gods and goddesses hate lies.

She was too young to confront such a dilemma — this was something a grown person should do. "I wish Father were . . ." Maïa started to say to Seti, but stopped when Aunt turned and fixed them with a piercing stare.

"Do not get lost. Do not eat bad food. Stay out of the sun when you can, and be home by dusk." Then she pushed through the crowd to join the priests' wives, all holding their sistrums. Maïa followed as best she could, with Seti and Ipi close by.

The crowd parted as the High Priest wrapped in his leopard skin came out of the temple door; following him were more priests bearing a wooden shrine on their shoulders. Maïa knew that hidden inside was the newly washed and dressed statue of their god Amun. She shivered with excitement. This was the time when their lives were joined to Amun's; his good fortune would be theirs. It would then be joined to the power of Hatshepsut — divine daughter of the god Amun — when they all met at the temple of Luxor.

At the end of the group of priests, Maïa thought she saw Uncle, walking woodenly, looking from side to side. Then the crowd began the great procession; first came the priests, then the women shaking their sistrums. By standing on tiptoe, Maïa could see Aunt; her face shone — with happiness?

Maïa kept as close as she could, fearing her aunt's displeasure if she fell behind. Then came the dancers, dark-skinned men from Nubia who made Maïa's feet lift and step in rhythm. Other people played flutes and many sang hymns of praise to the god while soldiers marched, banging on drums.

They all were part of a vast dance, Maïa thought, celebrating their god and the good fortune to come — rich harvests, plenty of food, and barley beer. *But how can there be good fortune when a priest steals and lies?*

Seti did not notice when Maïa stopped, wiping the sweat from her pale face. "Ah, I love festivals, I love ceremonies," Seti chattered beside her. "Afterward, they will give out beer and bread."

Suddenly, she heard her name called over the babble of voices, "Maïa! Over here!" She paused to see Meret running toward her with Pashed, her servant.

The girls clasped each other's hands. "Are you

all right?" Maïa asked. The tooth marks from the monkey's bite were seamed, still red, but not a hot swollen red. Meret nodded. "I am well."

"Ah," Maïa sighed.

"Mother is right over there." Meret pointed to her left, and Maïa saw Nefert, clothed in white linen, with a sparkling necklace of turquoise and red stones. She waved and smiled, pointing to her daughter's arm.

"My heart is happy to see you," Maïa said.

She introduced Seti and Meret, then slowed with the crowd as they reached one of the six resting places along the avenue to the Luxor temple.

The priests set down the god's barque and drank from water jars the temple servants offered them. The priests' wives rested as well, drinking water and wiping their brows. Seti, Maïa, and Meret stood off to the side, fanning one another's faces with their hands. She looked for Ipi but could not see her.

"Look!" Maïa pointed to her aunt, who was sitting down with some other women. The familiar frown was back.

"Who is she?" Meret said. "She looks very crabby."

"Ha! She is. That is my nothing-is-ever-good-enough-for-me-you-lazy-niece aunt!"

Meret held her wrist, and they stayed close together as the procession began once again, dancing, swirling, chanting, calling out as they neared the gleaming white temple of Luxor. Soon they were at the gate that led to the temple courtyard. Bright banners fluttered from tall poles, and two towering obelisks thrust to the sky, carved with hieroglyphs telling of Hatshepsut's power and great deeds.

"Sister, I cannot wait — now we will see her!" Seti stared eagerly ahead.

Meret gripped Maïa's hand; standing on tiptoe, they strained to catch sight of Hatshepsut.

The Horus, Might of Kas; the Golden Horus, Divine of Appearance; the Good Goddess, Lady of Two Lands, King of Upper and Lower Egypt, Maatkare; Daughter of Re, Hatshepsut, Beloved of Amun. Maïa said all of Her Majesty's names to herself. Only a woman of power, a great ruler, could wear the king's false beard and headdress. Only a woman of power could subdue rebellion, keep the robbers in the red desert, and bring peace and prosperity to Egypt. Perhaps *she* would welcome a girl who could write.

Maïa remembered something Father had once told her about the chariots used in warfare. They were harnessed by leather straps to fast horses, and the archers flew along in light chariots behind.

She wished that all her worries could be left behind, that she could harness her fortunes to Hatshepsut and follow in her glittering wake.

CHAPTER SEVEN

They were like a wave on the Nile, an inundation of people singing, dancing, calling out, and following the swaying shrine of the god Amun carried on poles by the priests. Maïa's heart thumped in rhythm to the soldiers drumming; the sacred songs fluted up and down her arms. She felt like someone else, not Maïa anymore. She forgot Aunt. She forgot Meret and Nefert nearby and her brother and Ipi. All she wanted was to see the face of Her Majesty.

The crowd slowed, crept forward, then halted. They had reached the white temple of Luxor. Leading up to it was a courtyard with sacred statues standing like guardians of Egypt — kings and Hatshepsut looking stern and protective. A bird soared overhead, and Maïa wondered how it could fly in the heat. Sweat coursed down her back, drenching her shift and the seal hidden within.

"There she is — Her Majesty!" people shouted.

The priests carrying the shrine of Amun had to force their way through the crowd; soldiers helped, pushing the people back. "Make room for the god and his priests!"

The shrine swayed from side to side, as if a wild wind blew. Then it stopped, with a shudder. All the voices suddenly stopped as well.

"Welcome to the temple of Luxor, my priests, Amun my father, and my people."

The voice was not large; it was not small. It was not fluting like an instrument, nor yet softly chiming like a sistrum. It was its own voice, full of authority and power and something sharp-edged, like the swept line of a desert dune.

Standing as tall as she could, Maïa still could not see Her Majesty. Almost crying with frustration, she jumped up and down beside a big soldier nearby who laughed and lifted her onto his back. "There, my daughter, take a good look at Maatkare!"

Then she could see her: small, slight, wearing the sacred headdress, the crown of Upper and Lower Egypt, and a false, braided beard. Her eyes were as dark and mysterious as a god's. Golden armbands circled her upper arms, and she wore the kilt of a king, the *shendyt,* with a gleaming gold apron in front. A large, jeweled pectoral with a blue-and-gold Eye of Horus covered her chest.

Maïa felt drawn to her, as if an invisible cord stretched from her over the gaping crowd to Her Majesty's arm. For a moment, Hatshepsut's head swiveled, and their eyes met. Then the soldier grunted, let Maïa slip to the ground, and hurried to watch Amun's shrine enter the temple.

"Did you see her, Maïa?" Seti jostled her elbow.

"Yes." Maïa could not say what she had seen.

"She is smaller than I thought she would be," Meret called, from her perch on Pashed's shoulders. "Much smaller, but beautiful." She slid to the ground.

"Hurry." Nefert took her daughter's arm. "This is the time; a few citizens can go into the temple to ask questions of the god. I want to ask Amun when my husband is coming home!" They pressed forward together.

The priests and the swaying barque went past tall pillars covered with sacred hieroglyphs, to the open doors of the temple. The barque paused for a moment, some words were said, and Hatshepsut, then the High Priest in his leopard skin, the sacred shrine, and all of the priests passed through the opening and disappeared into darkness.

A gong sounded. "Those with questions for the god may come forward — we will take only a few."

Follow! Make yourself one with the priests. Hurry!

Maïa unlinked her arms and darted through the crowd, thrusting with her sharp elbows. She was dimly aware of her friends just behind. Pushing against the bodies like a swimmer going upstream, Maïa reached the temple entrance. Soldiers shouted at the crowd, pointing to some and waving others away: "You, not you, you, not you!"

Without knowing how it happened, Maïa became one of the "you"; Meret, Nefert, and Seti those of the "not you," and she was swept into the quiet of the temple as the doors closed behind her. Incense pulsed in thick clouds toward the ceiling. Lights flickered along the sides of the stone room.

The priests set down the sacred barque, wiping their brows and heaving sighs of relief in the coolness. Watching intently, she saw a small group of Theban citizens ahead, mostly men and some women, all with questions for the god.

But before that could happen, there was one more sacred ritual to perform in secret. The priests lifted up the barque and bore the god off to an inner room of the temple.

Maïa heard murmurs, silence, then other softly spoken words. She imagined Her Majesty in the inner room, performing the secret rite that would, so Uncle said, ensure good harvest. Amun would fertilize their fields in the same way he impregnated Hatshepsut's mother with his divine child.

The incense swelled again, clouds disappearing in the dark ceiling. Doors opened from the inner room, and the shrine of Amun appeared once again, with Hatshepsut walking beside it.

A voice called out, "Theban citizens! This is your time to ask questions of our god. Ask, and you shall receive an answer. Remember: If the barque dips forward, that signifies a 'yes'; if the barque dips backward, that signals a 'no.'"

For a moment, the hard clay seal pressed against Maïa's skin; she adjusted the cord around her chest, but the clay still dug into her skin.

One man, well dressed, with a gold armband, inquired, "How is my brother in the Delta, O Amun?"

After a pause, the barque dipped forward, and

the man stepped back, clasping his hands. "He is well, this is good news indeed!"

A finely dressed woman called out, "Will my son recover from the Nile fever? He is so ill."

A slight beat — as of a stilled drum — and the barque dipped backward. The woman wailed, "I knew it, he is so frail, so weak!"

An elderly man asked after his estate in the Delta, "Will the inundation give me good crops this year? Should I plant emmer wheat or barley?"

The barque did not move, and a priest called out in an annoyed voice, "Only questions answered by a yes or a no will be allowed."

Then, as if a great hand pressed her forward, Maïa felt taller, and her heart seemed full of light. She spoke in a voice unlike her own, "O Amun, is my uncle Hay stealing grain from the temple of Karnak?"

There was a horrified silence, then whispers, and the barque suddenly dipped forward. Maïa stumbled, filled with the power of the god. He had spoken. Uncle was stealing grain, and his wickedness would bring down evil upon them all.

Somewhere an inhuman yowling went up, like a cat who has just been stepped on. Soldiers rushed toward a side wall of the temple, and from the corner of her eye, Maïa saw Uncle being hustled away.

She did not feel happy to see his flailing thin arms, his terrified face. With a sudden and awful jolt Maïa came back to herself: Where could she go now, and what would happen to her beloved brother?

Chapter Eight

There was a moment of silence that widened and stretched out around Maïa. She felt alone, marked, and began to tremble. But as the silence lapped at her feet, she felt the presence of Amun inside: *My child, you have done well*.

A priest grabbed her arm and hustled her into a side room of the temple. It was a man she had seen once or twice with Uncle Hay, a short, thick-bodied man with a face glistening with sweat. Maïa swayed from the strong, scented oil she wore.

"Drink!" The priest thrust a clay vessel at her, and she drank the tepid water, but it eased the dust in her throat. She remembered his name now — Paneb.

"You, girl — you nothing — how could you

suspect that one of our most respected priests is guilty of stealing temple grain? This is a serious charge!" He raised his hand and fixed her with his cold, dark eyes.

Maïa swallowed and looked around. She wished Meret and Seti were here.

She reached inside her shift, took out the temple seal, and wiped it hurriedly before giving it to the priest. *I belong to the temple of Karnak.* "I found this at the top of our storeroom stairs. There are five new sacks of grain inside that were not there the day before."

Paneb paced about the small room, rubbing his face. "But why would Hay take such a risk? He oversees the temple grain; he has everything to lose by stealing! This seal could be found by anyone, anywhere." He stopped and stared at her.

Maïa ducked her head, afraid of his eyes. They seemed naked and unattached, like the eyes of a beast plucked out by vultures. "I heard him, sir . . . that night, with our donkey. . . . Uncle was walking down the steps — his footsteps were heavy — and a day or two before, I saw a boat nosing into the reeds near our house."

Paneb coughed, rubbed his face again, and tapped

one hand against another. "If this is true — *if* — it will hurt the dignity of this temple, of Amun's priests. It still is not proven. . . . How can I present this to Her Majesty?" He seemed to be talking to himself. "But then, the god spoke when the barque dipped forward, and all saw that. Pah!" He summoned an underling standing against the wall. "Go to the house of the priest Hay and search his cellar for the stolen grain. Hurry!"

Then he turned to Maïa. His face looked weary and disgusted. "You — out of my sight, and I will keep . . . this." He hissed, closing his fist around the temple seal. "Remember, you troublemaker — telling the truth is not always the best thing!"

As she turned to go, he put out a hand. "Wait, go out by the back door. I will tell Her Majesty all she needs to know. If I ever see you again — vermin — things will go badly for you!" Before he shoved her out the door, one of Her Majesty's soldiers strode into the room.

"I am to take the girl to Maatkare, Her Majesty. Come with me." He grabbed Maïa's arm and led her away, as Paneb hopped up and down, hissing like a cobra.

If Maïa had not been so frightened, she would

have laughed. But now she had to tell her story to Hatshepsut! What if she did not believe her?

Knees trembling, Maïa walked with the soldier into a back room of the temple. Sitting at one end on a carved, elaborate chair was Hatshepsut, still wearing the sacred headdress and glittering kilt, but her false beard was gone. The blue-and-gold Eye of Horus in the royal pectoral seemed to stare at Maïa, accusing her of lying. The golden cobra on Her Majesty's headdress so frightened Maïa that no one had to tell her to prostrate herself; she fell to her knees, sinking facedown onto the stone floor.

"Rise, my child."

As she got to her feet, Maïa dared to glance at her, then away again. It was like looking at the sun — the shine on her skin, the gleam of gold, the aura of holiness and power that emanated from Hatshepsut.

"Tell me how you suspected that priest was stealing grain from our temple, girl."

After she had listened to the story, Her Majesty tapped one finger on the chair's arm. The golden rings on her fingers gleamed in the dim light.

"My Majesty knows the power the priests of Amun have at our temples, counselor." She turned and looked at a dark man in rich clothing to her left. "What if this girl has a grudge?"

Maïa stood straight and tall. In her thoughts, she saw the signs for *djedeni em maat*: "I have spoken in truth." She repeated the words, and it seemed Amun surrounded and upheld her.

"Ah." Hatshepsut let out a long breath. "That is the sound of truth speaking. Hapuseneb, counselor, what should be done? What is your name, girl?"

"Maïa," she answered softly.

The thin man with a hawk's nose bent and whispered in Her Majesty's ear, and Hatshepsut nodded. "Girl, Amun has said your uncle is guilty, but still his house must be searched so that justice, Maat, will be satisfied. Maïa, you did right to tell us of this wrong."

Hapuseneb held out a small, richly decorated purse. Hatshepsut reached in and drew out something, which she gave to Maïa.

A delicate gold shape glittered in her hand — a small feather like the one the goddess Maat wore. "I am not worthy of this great gift, Your Majesty, but I thank you!"

Hatshepsut said, "It is fitting that a feather of

the goddess of truth and justice be your reward, Daughter. Remember — the priests of Amun are jealous guardians of their honor!"

Holding the gold feather, Maïa backed out of the room, not daring to glance at her ruler again. She turned, looking only at the tall doors beyond; she would not look at the priests assembled there, and would not look one in the eye.

Through the door she hurried into the blinding sun, which hit her like a hand. She felt light-headed, like one who has drunk too much wine, and her stomach churned. Someone grabbed her arm, and Maïa screamed.

"Hush, it is only Meret. Are you all right?"

"Oh, Meret, I fear . . . I fear . . ." The sky darkened, the dust in her throat rose up, and Maïa sank to the ground.

"Hold her up, I say," came a commanding voice. Nefert knelt beside her, with Seti on her other side. "Tell me what happened inside, child."

"I — I — asked a question of the god in the sacred barque. . . ." Maïa tried to swallow but could not. Seti fanned his hands over her face to cool her.

"And?" Nefert asked impatiently. Her tall

servant, Pashed, kept a space cleared about them at the side of the courtyard of the temple.

She forced the words out of her mouth. "The barque dipped forward. It is the truth. My uncle *was* stealing grain from the temple."

Seti jumped up. "No, he would not, that is sacrilege, Maïa! The punishments are terrible!"

Maïa's head throbbed; she feared she might be sick. Seti was angry with *her,* not with Uncle Hay!

"Keep back," Nefert commanded, as her eyes glittered, and she smiled slightly. "Pashed, take her up — we must get her away. . . . Seti?" But Seti had disappeared into the crowd, along with Ipi, and could not be seen.

Maïa felt herself lifted up and hurried out of the crowd. The air was blasting hot, and the cries and chants of the crowd continued as if nothing had happened inside the temple, as if she had not, herself, spoken to the god and received an answer.

CHAPTER NINE

In the dark room of the inn, an oil lamp flickered. All the windows were open to catch whatever breeze there was. Meret sat on one sleeping mat, with Maïa slumped against her. She seemed to need support, as if the afternoon had sucked out all her strength and will. Nefert sat opposite, eyeing Maïa.

"Child, you are safe with us — no one knows you are here. The innkeeper thinks I have two daughters." She smiled at Maïa. "And so I have two daughters again."

"But, Mistress . . ."

"Nefert!" She took off her gold armband and handed it to her servant.

"Mistress Nefert . . . I do not think I can call

you . . ." Words felt dry and hard as pellets of clay in her mouth.

"Call me Nefert." The woman tilted her head as the servant combed her hair back, then wiped her face with a wet cloth.

"Maïa, are you useful in some way?"

"Useful, Mistress?" Maïa cleared her throat.

Meret gave her a quizzical glance; she knew that Maïa could make signs, and she made little pushing motions with her hands, to encourage Maïa.

"I can write some," she finally said. "I was taught hieroglyphs by my brother, Seti — and, oh, Mistress Nefert, we must try to find him! What if Paneb harms him? He threatened me!"

"Not now, Maïa. We must leave before morning light and get you out of Thebes, until the memory of the god answering a young girl's question is forgotten."

"I do not think that will ever be forgotten," Meret said. She took a sip of wine, then held the cup out to Maïa. The sweet, heavy wine did not wash away her thirst.

"I hope they do not forget. Let them remember the corruption of their priests, useless charlatans!"

At a glance from her daughter, Nefert stopped

and put her hands to her flushed cheeks. "Sleep now, girls. We will leave early tomorrow by boat."

As Maïa lay down, she finally uncurled her fingers to look again at the miniature feather. Delicately, she traced the curling gold shape, then sighed. She, Maïa, a useless niece and troublemaker had a present from Hatshepsut! She tucked it inside her cloth amulet bag, beside the small figure of smiling Bes.

Before she slept, she heard Nefert whispering, "An enemy of the priests of Amun!"

The crew shouted as the sail was pulled up, bellying in the wind. The sail tautened, swelled, and the boat leaped forward against the current, south along the dark river. In front, one man looked ahead; in back, a thickly muscled servant steered the boat with a long oar. Nefert rested on cushions in the middle of the boat under a striped awning, while the two girls sat, heads together.

Maïa sighed with pleasure; to be going upriver, a fresh wind in her face, away from her nagging aunt and the disgrace of her uncle! If only Seti were with her! She looked up at the gray sky where Sopdet shone brightly. Was Seti looking at the same star and thinking of her?

"All will be well, friend," Meret yawned. "You will be safe with us."

"That may be so," Maïa said, "and I am grateful to your mother, but I am worried about my brother, and I had no time to say good-bye to Ipi before we left."

"Who is Ipi?" Meret leaned against a cushion.

"My aunt's servant. When Aunt yelled at me, she was always kind, and she had courage."

"Tell me about her."

Maïa turned to her. "Once when she was washing laundry in the river, a crocodile seized her foot, and she thumped the washing stone on his eye!"

Meret clapped her hands. "Brave indeed. We could use such a one in my mother's household."

Why is bravery needed in your house? Maïa wondered, looking over at Nefert. The breeze lifted her hair from her face, and for a moment, as the woman stared over the water, she looked sad.

"Mother admires courage." Meret offered Maïa a date. "Father is an officer in Her Majesty's army, often away. That man can fight lions with a single spear!"

Meret began to chant a poem of triumph: of a

man striding out across the hot desert sands, lying in wait for the greatest of beasts, finally driving a spear deep into the bloody heart of the lion.

"He told my mother that he ate the lion's heart."

"Ugh." Maïa sat up straighter.

"He said it did not taste very good but, then, courage may taste more like metal than flowers or pomegranates." She shrugged her shoulders.

Maïa was sure her father had never feasted on the heart of a killed lion. On carp, perhaps, on river swimmers, ducks, and roasted geese, but not a lion. He was too gentle to have ever wanted that.

A slight breeze ruffled Maïa's hair as the sun rose, casting red rays over the river ahead. Before the boat rounded a bend, Maïa turned to look back. There lay Thebes, glittering, beautiful Thebes, the only home she'd ever had. It had given birth to her and Seti; had given her a laughing mother and a handsome father; and it had taken them away, dry as a mummy. It had given her an orphan home with no words of love. Now she was leaving for an estate south of Thebes, a day's journey, Nefert assured her, and close to the river's cool breezes. What would her new home be like, and how could she visit Seti?

As the boat went farther upriver, more craft appeared on the water: low sloops carrying cargo, the elegant wooden boats of nobles with awnings set up to shield the passengers, and the small reed skiffs of fishermen. Maïa could hear them calling to each other, their voices sailing like bright birds.

At midday, Pashed brought out bowls filled with dates, figs, chunks of bread, and flasks of wine. As she ate, Maïa looked over at Nefert, who regarded her with a baffling expression. Was it the way her uncle looked at their donkey?

Meret threw the date pits into the water, complaining of the heat, but Maïa thought only the crew could complain, as she watched sweat rolling off their faces.

The two girls curled up on cushions under the awning and slept as the wind blew, boats sailed past, and the sun traveled from east to west. When Maïa woke, the sun's rays struck the red cliffs on the western bank, and the boat headed toward its landing dock.

The girls got up and peered over the side of the boat. "That's Mother and Father's land." Meret pointed to the partially flooded fields. Date palms waved in the hot wind, and a flock of birds whirred overhead. A floating dock awaited them, and the oarsman leaned hard on the oar as the crew let down the sail. The man in front jumped onto the dock and tied up the boat.

Pashed put two planks from the deck to the platform below and helped Nefert to her feet. Stretching like a cat, she shook her hair back. "Ah, home — at last."

"Hurry, Maïa, hurry! I am starving and sweaty and I need a bath now!" Meret ran down the planks, laughing at the sound her sandals made on the wood, and Maïa followed.

There was an air of calm, of well-being to these fields with irrigation ditches for the water farther up and mud dikes to contain the floods. They walked across the edge of one field to a series of low, white buildings.

Pashed opened the gate to the courtyard and ushered them in, calling, "Chety, we are home!"

A short woman with gray hair and gentle eyes came to greet them. "Welcome home, Mistress. Did you have a good trip? How was the festival?" Her eyes widened at the sight of Maïa.

"All went well, Chety. We have a visitor — well, more a new relation." Nefert laughed gaily. "This is my new daughter, Maïa. She has accused a priest in the temple of Amun of stealing grain, and we are giving her refuge. Come!" She motioned with her hand, but before Maïa followed, she looked about the well-kept courtyard: at the pools of shadow and the blue lotus floating on a pool that shimmered in the last light.

Maïa went through the door and gasped. The floor of the main room was covered with red and blue tiles, and the walls were painted with green reeds and a decorative border. She had heard of such houses, but had never seen one. It felt cool, restful, as if nothing bad could ever happen here.

"Ah, home!" Meret spread her arms wide. "Come on, Maïa. Let us bathe before we eat."

They walked through several rooms before coming to a chamber with two high windows and a tiled floor. There was a real bed with a wooden frame and a small wooden headrest and with a carved chest against the wall.

"That would be for your clothes, Maïa, except you do not have any. But Mother will make certain you have enough shifts and cloaks for winter."

"Winter," Maïa whispered. It seemed so far away. They were at the beginning of the New Year, with heat as heavy as cedar limbs, and the river rising. Winter was far away, full of lucky and unlucky days; full of time to fail and get into trouble.

"Why are you clutching your middle, Maïa? You do not like it here?"

"I like it, Meret, and I am grateful to your mother, it is just . . . I did not think, when I told the priest of my uncle's wickedness . . ." Her voice sank.

Meret pulled her down onto the side of the bed. "Hush. You worry too much. I will teach you to be happier, to sing more." She opened her mouth and began one of the sweet chants to Amun's glory. Her voice reminded Maïa of her mother, but when Maïa tried to join in, her voice wavered.

When they were done, Meret tapped her lightly on her arm. "Come." She slipped out of her shift and left it on the bed. Maïa did the same, taking off the small bag with her amulet and the gold feather.

Next door was a small room paved with stone. A young girl awaited them, holding out clay jars with moisture beaded along their sides.

"Ah!" Meret held up her arms as the servant poured cool water over her. Meret took up a bunch of softened reeds, dipped them in the paste of desert salt and water, and scrubbed her body. When she was all rinsed, she stepped aside.

Maïa had never been bathed by anyone except her mother, and she felt too shy to lift her arms the way Meret did — as if she owned a piece of the sky, as if she had the right to be here, under this water.

Hurriedly, Maïa scrubbed herself as the water rained down. She thought, *Oh, Aunt, if you could see me now, being taken care of like a true noble. Seti, I wish you could see me in this wonderful house with a real bed.*

Then, overcome at the thought of her brother, she traced the image of an eye with tears flowing out. Somehow, the shape eased her sorrow.

"Maïa!" her friend snapped. "Be careful! That almost got you into trouble with Mother that day at market. If you must write picture signs, do so on a piece of pottery or in the dirt, but not in the air like an evil person making spells."

Maïa gulped, took the linen cloth the servant girl held out, and rubbed herself dry. She would have to be careful, but who would teach her? How could she find a place for herself in this rich house, surrounded by unanswered questions and mysterious looks from Nefert?

CHAPTER TEN

Maïa slept and woke and slept again. The bed felt constraining; she was used to the freedom of a mat on a roof, out under the stars. Here four walls surrounded her, and though there was a slight breeze from the vents, it was still hot. Each time she woke, she thought of Seti: Was he wondering where *she* was? What had happened to him? In her whole life they had never before been separated. She felt as if half of herself were missing.

Just before dawn, Maïa finally slept, exhausted, only to wake to the jolting of her bed.

"How did you sleep, my new sister? Well, I hope?" Meret's kind smile warmed Maïa.

"I thought of Seti," Maïa answered softly.

"You miss him, just the way I miss my sister,

Nesty." But before Maïa could ask about her, a girl appeared and handed a damp linen cloth to Maïa.

She rubbed her face with it awkwardly. It was too much, too soon. At home she would have been up, practicing writing with Seti. Then she would have helped Ipi make breakfast, with no servants in sight except Ipi and herself.

"It is that . . ." She handed the wet cloth back to the girl. "I am not used to all of this."

"But your uncle was a priest. Surely, you did not live like workers in the fields?"

"Of course not! But Uncle was miserly and would not hire any more servants. He said they cost too much. So I was . . . a servant," she finished softly.

"That will change here, be certain of that! Now." Meret extended a hand and pulled Maïa upright. "Here is a dress Mother told me to give you." She held a soft linen shift above Maïa's head, helping her to slip it on. "And here is something to go with it." She held out an armband of bright red and blue beads.

She protested, "But this is too rich for me!"

Meret put her hand over Maïa's mouth. "Stop saying that or I shall be angry! Mother has plans for you — I do not know what they are, but we will find out. Besides, this is a dress my mother had made for

Nesty, who never wore it, for she died two years ago of a fever. The priests told her it was demons, the same men who could not cure my sister, who only chanted spells and waved snake wands over her. Pah!"

Maïa plucked uncertainly at the shift; she was not sure she wished to wear the dress of Meret's dead sister, but did she have a choice? Now she knew why Nefert's voice was glad when she had murmured, "An enemy of the priests of Amun!"

"My mother has no use for priests now. She is still bitter. Come." They walked through Meret's bedroom, through another room, to the painted chamber where they ate yesterday. Nefert sat in a chair carved with lotus buds.

"There you are. Did you sleep well, my daughter?" She looked intently at her clothing and jewelry.

Maïa shivered. She knew that Nefert meant well, but she wished she could have refused to wear the shift. "I thank you for this dress and armband." Maïa gestured at both. What was the right tone to take with her? Grateful thanks? Respectful distance?

"Come sit by me." The woman gestured at a wooden stool nearby.

Maïa sat and watched a servant set down dishes of sliced cucumbers, grapes, and warm bread on a small table. Another servant brought a flagon of cool barley beer. Maïa picked at the grapes.

"Maïa, eat! It makes me sad to give you all these things and have you be unhappy," Nefert said.

"I am grateful, Lady. . . ."

"Call me Nefert, not 'Lady' like a servant!"

"Yes, Mistress — yes, Nefert." She nibbled on a slice of cucumber and plucked at her dress.

"First of all, tell me of your life and what happened to you up to the day we met in the market, where you were making signs in the air. Were you not?"

Maïa lowered her eyes. "Yes, you can only do it with a few words, but it was a secret language of Brother and me, for Uncle was often displeased with me."

She went on to tell Nefert and Meret how she had been the beloved daughter of two parents and the loved sister of Seti; how they had been happy in their small house in Thebes where Father was a craftsman; how her parents had died of the fever, and she and Seti had come to Aunt and Uncle's house. . . .

"They died of a fever, you say?" Nefert thumped her cup of wine onto the table. "Did you call in the priests to heal your parents?"

"No, Lady . . . Nefert, we did not — it all happened so fast."

"Go on, go on. Tell us the rest of your tale."

Maïa spoke of living with her aunt and uncle: how she heard Uncle at night, found the sacks of stolen grain and the temple seal; and how she gave it to the priest. *Only two days ago.*

"Ha! He was not happy to get that seal from you!" Nefert seized the cup and drank deeply.

"No, Paneb was not. He frightened me."

"What did he say to you?" Meret asked.

"He called me a troublemaker and said it was not always wise to tell the truth." Maïa remembered the power of the man, the strength that flowed from him as he confronted her.

"Well, he cannot harm you here, Daughter. All will be different and you will be a valued daughter of the house." She clapped her hands, and the woman with the gray hair and gentle eyes appeared. "Chety, bring me some shards and the scribe's kit."

Maïa wondered how the lady came to have a scribe's kit. Most did not own them, unless they had scribes in their houses or worked at the temple.

"My overseer can write," Nefert explained. "And it is very useful for keeping accounts of our estate, the crops, and all of that. But I do not always wish him to write my private letters to my husband."

Chety came noiselessly into the room, laying down a narrow piece of pottery on the table by Maïa, along with the palette containing two circles filled with hardened ink. With a slight click, the servant put down a small dish of water and a reed brush.

"Now, begin." Nefert eyed Maïa. "Write as if you were writing to your brother in Thebes." Meret stood behind her shoulder.

Maïa felt oppressed by their presence, their hopes. If she wrote poorly, would she have to leave and cease being the "new daughter" of the house?

Licking her lips, she dipped the brush into the water and swept it across the black ink until it was dark, the way Seti had taught her. Pulling the shard closer, she wrote her brother's name, as if addressing a letter, and read it aloud as she wrote from the right side of the piece to the left.

My dear brother, I miss you and am sad. I am safe with friends. I long to have news of you. Maïa. Her chest hurt so much that she had to press one hand to it.

Nefert cried, "That is wonderful!" She tilted the inscribed piece from side to side. "It looks just like the letters my overseer has written."

Maïa gave her a dark glance, like a child who has seen another receive a sweet while she got none.

"Thank you, Lady — my brother taught me well." She bit her lip. "I am so worried about him. What if he is being punished with my uncle?"

"I cannot have my scribe being unhappy." Nefert rose and patted Maïa's shoulder. "Shall I send a servant to Thebes to find out what has happened to Seti?"

"Oh, yes, such a kindness! If only I knew."

"It shall be done."

Then Meret took the pottery piece and looked hard at it, at Maïa, then back to the black hieroglyphs. Her eyes only widened at the writing.

Taking Maïa by the arm, Meret led her outside by the pool to sit under reed shades. Near the water sat a tall cat, tail switching. At the sudden splash of a frog, the cat leaped and came down in one place.

"Ha! He is always trying to catch the frog, and he never can!" Meret laughed and drew Maïa down beside her on dry ground. "Silly cat, silly Miw."

"Oh, that was our cat's name."

"I guess it is a common one. Now, my friend, would you teach me to write? If we are to be sisters, please show me the signs."

Maïa paused. "What will your mother think?"

Meret shook her head. "Let us keep it a secret for now, until I can surprise her."

Maïa sighed and plucked at the pleated dress, finer than anything she had ever had. She owed them so much. "Of course I will teach you, for you and your mother got me out of Thebes and gave me a home. Aunt would never have let me inside her house again! And Paneb said some evil words before I left."

"Well, we helped you, and you rescued me from that vicious monkey! We are even now — there is no debt." Meret placed her cool fingers on Maïa's arm, and something passed through her skin that felt like a welcome.

CHAPTER ELEVEN

Maïa thrashed in her bed. The air from the roof vents did not reach her. Sweat pooled on her skin, and no amount of waving a fan could cool her. Horrible pictures filled her head: of Seti, desperately running away; of Uncle with a bloodied stump for an arm; of Ipi, wailing a hymn of grief. *You had to tell the truth. You put Seti in harm's way and destroyed Aunt's family.*

Jumping out of bed, she trailed out to the reflecting pool, and lay down on dry ground. It was a little cooler, and she did not feel the four walls closing in, suffocating her. Gently touching Hatshepsut's gift, she prayed for her strength and courage.

A rustling frightened her, and she sat up, hugging her knees. "Who's there?" she quavered.

A slight *prrrt!* answered her, and the cat walked up, tail high. He butted her hand, sniffed her skin, then curled up beside her. "Oh, Miw!" Maïa let her hand rest on his back; he would protect her.

She dreamed of Mother, singing and opening the clay jar for new notes like swift birds: purple, gold, silver, and green, they floated through the air and dove into the jar.

This is for bravery, Maïa. Her mother caught a purple note. *And this is for understanding.* She pressed the golden note against Maïa's forehead. *Green is for new life, and do not forget the silver. It shows you are a child of Amun, who will protect you. Go softly, my daughter, without fear.*

For the first time in days, Maïa woke without her eyes and mouth pinched with worry. She looked at the sun rising and wished on a bird darting overhead. Perhaps it was a good omen for Nefert's servant, Merisu, and his trip to Thebes to find Seti.

Merisu had left late yesterday, as the fierceness of the sun lessened. Maïa told him how to recognize her brother: "He looks like me, but with a crescent moon mark here. . . ." She pressed a finger on her right shoulder. Then she gave him directions to her uncle's house, while Chety put small pieces of jewelry into a bag for buying information.

Merisu took one of the estate's donkeys to ride the day's journey to Thebes, for Nefert did not want him to travel alone by boat on the river.

As the two girls watched the donkey trotting out of sight down the road, Maïa protested, "I wish your mother were sending someone else — he is so small." She did not add that his skin looked like melted wax and that he had no eyebrows.

"Mother says he is fast, discreet, and she has used him before. Do not ask me for what, because I do not know. Stop worrying!"

But that next morning, as Maïa sat by the reflecting pool, she worried that something had happened to Merisu: The donkey had run away, robbers had set upon him, or he had decided to never return. Her fretting was interrupted by a cheerful call from the doorway.

"Maïa! I looked for you in your room, but I see you slept outside." Meret came and sat beside her friend. "You were not afraid of scorpions or snakes?"

"Not when Miw is here to protect me." Maïa stroked the cat and was rewarded with a long purr.

"Miw is a good guardian." Fondly, Meret rubbed the cat's ears, then she rose, holding out her hand. "Come, Maïa, shall we go fishing on the river?"

Maïa grinned suddenly. "I have not done that since Father died. Uncle would never take me, for he feared the hippos and the crocodiles."

"Well, he should fear them. But if we are careful, no harm will come to us."

Telling Nefert where they were going, Meret led Maïa to the back of the house, where a servant was making bread in the courtyard. Maïa felt a sudden pang — so often Ipi and she had mixed the dough in a wooden trough, let it rise, then stuffed it into clay molds to bake on the coals.

"Are you missing your brother again, Maïa?" Meret put her hand on her arm. "Some food will cheer you." Meret persuaded Teti, the servant, to give them some bread and dates. Sticking them into a sack with a water flask, the girl led the way to the river. Pashed followed to help, and skittering along near his feet walked Miw, tail held high.

Water rose above the banks and flooded the edges of Nefert's fields. A few ibis made their way carefully, poking their long beaks into the water.

The air was thick and heavy with the smell of the river. Small birds skimmed the water, feeding on insects, and a sudden large splash startled Maïa.

She gripped Meret's arm. "Crocodile!"

"But we shall be safe in our boat and need not fear that monster."

Maïa did not want her friend to think her a coward, for Meret said that bravery was important in her house. Maïa wanted to be admired, to be something other than "a useless girl, a troublemaker."

The servant led them up to the floating dock and pulled close a slim wooden skiff with a paddle. "Climb in, Mistress; watch for crocodiles, and do not go too far."

"Yes, Pashed. No, Pashed," Meret said, as she lowered herself into the skiff. "Sit in front, Maïa, if you want to try fishing."

Maïa climbed in quickly, balancing on her knees as the boat rocked. Although she had not been out fishing since her parents died, the motion of the boat and the glint of sun on the river calmed her.

Miw stood on the dock, switching his tail and regarding them with a steady gaze. Suddenly, he took one long leap, landing in the front of the boat.

Meret exclaimed, "He is determined to protect us!" Laughing, she pushed off with the tall wooden paddle, and the boat sailed into the current.

Maïa was happy there were no papyrus thickets nearby that could hide hippos. For she remembered Father's story about a hippo rising up under a friend's boat, dumping the fisherman into the water, then dragging him under and killing him.

"We will not stay out long, but for a time, we can just be Meret and Maïa, not almost-women who will be married soon one day." Meret paddled hard, and the skiff wobbled in the current.

The cat peered into the river, his tail lashing as if he believed he could jump into the Nile, catch a fish, and jump back into the boat. Maïa was glad of his company; it reminded her of Father setting out in his boat with their cat perched in front.

She leaned closer over the water. Below, in the flowing depths, swam carp and river perch. Maïa held the net out the way Father had taught her, with a small club nearby in the bottom of the boat.

Meret cautioned, "Do not lean too far over the edge, or I shall have to rescue you."

Maïa laughed. "I *never* need rescuing when I am

in a boat, my second home!" For the first time in a long while, she felt like herself, as if she filled out her own skin.

Something broke the surface nearby, and Maïa motioned to Meret to steer the boat closer. They waited patiently as birds skimmed past and, farther downriver, they heard a hippo bellowing.

Maïa fingered her amulets. "Stay away, hippo!" A second time a fish broke the surface, and Maïa scooped him up in the net and clubbed him.

"How quick you are! We will give it to Teti, and she will season it with cumin and garlic, wrap it in lettuce, and serve it with lentils. Mmmm."

Miw butted the fish with his head and mewed.

"Do not let him eat it!" Paddling steadily, she headed the boat back home, singing a love song.

> *When I saw you*
> *My heart was caught*
> *Like a fish in a net*
> *Your breath, your lips*
> *Entrap me forever. . . .*

"Do you think that is how it happens, Maïa?" Meret paused, and silver drops ran off the paddle's edge.

"What?"

"That you see your beloved and both your hearts are caught like that fish in the net?"

Maïa watched an ibis fly slowly along shore. "I know nothing of love, Meret." *I have been too busy living with harsh words and heartache.*

"Well, I hope for a glorious life, full of rich food, beautiful clothing, a man who loves me, and healthy children — none who die of fever."

Maïa shook her head as the skiff nudged the side of the floating dock. Sickness was a mystery; sometimes the doctors helped, but often they could not. Her only plan was to be safe, to be reunited with Seti, and to be someone other than a "useless girl." Could her dream of being a scribe be found in this house? Dare she trust that?

CHAPTER TWELVE

"Where is my new daughter?"

Maïa barely heard as she stood on one leg, peering down the way to Thebes the next morning. That puff of dust coming toward her, was it Merisu? He could not be returning so soon, but her yearning to see Seti was like a rope flung toward Thebes; it would draw him back to her, with Merisu.

"Maïa? Where are you? Mother is calling for you!" Meret ran to the gate, motioning to Maïa.

Out of the puff of dust rode an elderly man on his donkey, past the path leading to Nefert's house.

"Maïa!"

She took one last, longing look down the road, then turned and waved to Meret. "I am coming."

"Hurry! Mother wants you." And Maïa ran into the courtyard, past the reflecting pool, into the house.

"Ah, there you are!" Nefert held out her rouged hands to her. "Please write a letter for me."

Maïa sat on a stool and drank some wine, trying to slow her breathing. "Whatever you wish."

"Whatever I wish," Nefert repeated almost mockingly. "What I wish is for you to write to my husband at the garrison near the first cataract, so far away." She sighed, and her face was etched with lines from her nose down to her chin.

"Mother means she misses Father." Meret plucked a fig from a dish and chewed on it. "He has not been home in a whole year, and that is too long."

"Her Majesty wants a peaceful Egypt, one without wars or rebellion." Nefert pushed away the food. "So our soldiers must always be ready to put down rebellion. My husband, Mekhu, is a trusted officer, so he is away and I am lonely."

She rose so suddenly that the table crashed on its side. Maïa jumped up to right it, picking up the scattered dates, but she stopped at a sharp look from Nefert.

"Let Chety do it! You betray your origins when you do so — did not your uncle have servants?"

Maïa ducked her head and sat. "Only one, Mistress, but I was more a servant than my uncle's niece."

"What a foolish man and a thief, too. You are well out of that house. From now on, to please me, do not clean or pick up anymore. Come outside, girls."

Maïa wondered if she could ever walk so elegantly. Would she ever have the palms of her hands rouged, like Nefert? They looked beautiful, like flowers at the ends of her arms.

Outside, in the shaded garden, three bright red cushions were arranged on the swept ground. As Nefert sat gracefully, arranging her shift about her legs, Maïa tried to imitate her, but sat with a thump — unlike Meret.

"Chety! The scribe's kit!" Nefert called.

The servant walked soundlessly out under the arbor, setting down the small tray with two ink blocks, a flask of water, reed brush, and papyrus. Catching her amazed look, Maïa thought that Chety had never known that women could write.

Maïa dipped her brush into the water and stroked it over the black ink. Trying to keep her hand from trembling, Maïa asked, "What would you like me to say?"

Meret eyed her with the same look Chety had just given her — wondering, respectful, and a trifle jealous.

"Tell my husband that I yearn for his embraces, that I am sorrowful he is gone, and that I am like a withered fig without him." Nefert paused. "Can you write all that to Mekhu?"

Maïa coughed nervously. "I think so, although I am not sure of the spelling for either 'fig' or 'embrace.' Could I use the word 'love' instead?"

Nefert nodded and sipped a cup of wine. Chety made excuses to stay with them, straightening the reed shades overhead and picking up dry leaves.

My dear husband, Maïa began, *I am like a dry well without your love. I am as withered as a dead frog without water. And my eyes weep because you are not here.*

She wrote the sounds for the word "weep" and ended with the final sign, an eye with drops spilling over the eyelid. Suddenly, she raised her head, aware of someone close behind her.

"That is like magic," Meret exclaimed. "As if the signs were locked in your fingers and then they flow through the brush to the papyrus."

Maïa held the brush up to let Meret know she had not forgotten her promise — to teach her to write. Then she bent her head, waiting for more instructions.

"Tell my husband there is a new daughter of the house, and you are the one writing this letter. Tell him the heat lies heavy on our land, that my heart is heavy also, and I yearn for his return. Tell him about priests of Amun . . ." Her voice trailed off.

When Maïa looked up, she was amazed to see the same drops of moisture dripping from Nefert's kohl-rimmed eyes, sliding down her face.

"I will write all of that." This time Maïa swept the brush across red ink, separating her words from Nefert's, and continued: *I am that daughter who writes to you now. My name is Maïa. The priests of Amun are angry with me, a scribe.*

Maïa made the hieroglyph for "scribe," drawing the palette with two ink circles, a pot of water, and a brush. Her heart beat strongly as she looked at the sign again. In black, she wrote: *The heat is heavy as is my heart. I am impatient for your return, my beloved.*

"There!" Maïa set her brush down, after writing "your loving wife" at the end. Nefert would never know that she had not written her exact words, for

Maïa did not know all of them. She wrote what she knew, translating Nefert's wishes and heart thoughts. Mekhu would know that he was loved, and that was all that mattered.

For a moment, Maïa wondered if she were twisting the truth, in a way the gods would hate. She drew in a breath, reading the letter silently. But she had written the sense of Nefert's words: Surely, that was telling the truth?

The woman rose gracefully, and held out her hand for the papyrus. "Oh, marvelous! I have my own scribe now — just like one of those useless, fake priests of Amun — who can send my heart wishes flying over the red desert to my husband. Thank you!"

She patted Maïa's cheek and turned to go inside. Chety followed, looking over her shoulder at Maïa as if she were an exotic animal from the land of Punt.

"Well." Meret clapped her hands. "You pleased my mother, Maïa. She will send a servant with this letter to find a boat going upriver to the first cataract. And after many days my father will open the papyrus, read Mother's words, and be comforted." She paused. "If we had not met each other that day in the market — if that monkey had not bitten me . . ." She shivered and traced the seamed scar.

"I know," Maïa said. "The ways of the gods are mysterious."

Meret nodded. "They are. Now that Mother is gone, teach me one word, Maïa."

"Do you think she will be angry, Meret? About your learning to write?"

"I do not know. My father used to say that more women could read and write in the old days of Egypt, so maybe he thinks it is a good thing. Mother likes it that you can write. When I can do a few hieroglyphs, then we can tell her."

"Then bring me a shard of pottery, Meret."

When she returned, they moved deeper into the shade of the palm trees. Maïa showed her friend how to dip the reed brush into water, shake off the excess, and stroke it across the black ink.

"What word do you want to learn, Meret?"

Her friend looked down, brows drawn together. Then she raised her eyes to Maïa and said firmly, "'Friend'! I wish to write the sign for 'friend,' *ak-ib.*"

"'One who has entered the heart,'" Maïa said. "It is a beautiful sign with the bird hieroglyph" — she wrote that — "a hillside, a pair of walking legs, the heart hieroglyph, and a seated woman, for us." Maïa wrote the signs representing different sounds on the clay shard; then she had Meret practice, using water and a leaf to rub out the first shaky lines, until she had written it clearly.

Meret held it up high in the light, squinted at it, and sighed with pleasure. "Thank you, friend!"

Maïa remembered the first word Seti had ever taught her — "woman" — and how she had written it over and over again, before her brother had finally said, "Yes, good." How excited she had been, how proud, just the way Meret was now.

She stood to follow Meret, taking a last look at the reflecting pool with the blue lotus. Father had told her the world began long ago with just such a lotus. In the warm sun, slowly its petals unfolded, showing the sun god in its middle. A sweet perfume drifted across the water. She was like that flower, slowly unfolding with light streaming out of her center. She was a scribe.

Chapter Thirteen

When she was not teaching Meret new signs, Maïa spent the next days wandering from room to room, praying to Bes, Hathor, and Amun, and standing on the road, looking for Merisu. As each day passed, she worried more and more about her brother.

"What do you think the priests will do to Uncle Hay?" she asked Nefert daily. To her reply that she did not know — it could be exile to one of the oases or some mutilation of the body — Maïa pressed her hand to her mouth. *Father told me of exile — the sands of the desert spread around the oasis and keep people prisoner.*

Then she would ask Meret, "What will I do if Merisu cannot find my brother?" Meret, although sympathetic, had no answer for that.

"Patience, child," Nefert told her, but Maïa was convinced time was running out like the drops of water dripping out of the water clock, marking the hours.

On the morning of the fourth day after Merisu left, she rose early, unable to sleep. Her hair stuck to the headrest of her bed, and hardly any air came into her room. As she tiptoed past Meret's room, Maïa looked in. Meret slept peacefully, like someone with no worries. Maïa wished to be like her.

Passing the pool with the frog, Maïa wished on it that today would bring news of Seti. Out on the road to Thebes, she watched the clouds in the east flare yellow, then pink. Birds called in the trees, as if they, too, wished to be active before the heat of the day, when their calls would be sullen and few.

Standing on tiptoe in her new sandals, Maïa tried to see down the dusty way. She heard the sound of a donkey's hoofs pattering. Around the corner came a man riding on the beast. He called a greeting as he went past, but he was not Merisu.

As the light widened, a party of travelers appeared: two men on donkeys, servants beside, and two elegant ladies in shaded litters. No one called a greeting to the girl standing by the road this time.

The dust settled, and Maïa sighed. This was a foolish errand, anyone could see that! But then, a small figure appeared in the distance. It seemed to be a lone traveler on a donkey, dust puffing up. Could it be Merisu? Maïa ran down the road, arms pumping.

"Was he there? Did you find him?" she shouted out, but when the person came closer, she saw he was an old man with a shining bald head.

"Yes, Daughter?" He stopped his donkey.

"Have you news, O Elder One?"

"Of what, my daughter?"

"Of Thebes, of the priest Hay who was accused in the temple, of news about his nephew, Seti." Maïa wrung her hands together.

The old man seized on the two words he recognized. "There is the trial in Thebes of the priest Hay from the Karnak temple. Is that who you mean?"

"Yes, yes, him, them! Tell me all!"

"I do not know very much, Daughter, only that he is up before the Theban court. They look for a witness, his niece." He peered at her with a kindly look.

"And of his nephew, do you know anything?"

"No, Daughter. Now, I must hurry, for my own

daughter, Tia, expects me." He kicked the donkey, and they set off at a trot, the grumble of the animal's empty stomach echoing in Maïa's ears.

Dust coated Maïa's lips. They were searching for a witness. What should she do? She fingered her Bes amulet and prayed for protection. Then she touched the edges of the curled golden feather, Hatshepsut's gift. She was a woman of courage, of vision. What would *she* do?

But there was no sense of the god within — no words came through the dawn, only the barking of a dog far away. Maïa went back to the courtyard to sit by the pool with the blue lotus.

If Seti were here, they would joke about Aunt's dreams. He would teach her more hieroglyphs and touch her hand gently when Uncle scolded her. Maïa felt as if a hole had opened up in her chest, and only the sight of her brother could fill it.

Meret and Nefert were still not awake; the first beams of the sun were shining across the courtyard when Maïa came to a decision.

"Even so." She tossed a leaf to the fat frog. "Even so, I will do it."

The day dragged by, hours filled with having her hair combed by Meret's servant and having her eyebrows plucked.

"Ouch! Why are we doing this?"

"So handsome men will fall in love with us, just as that fish was caught in your net, Maïa." Meret grimaced as the servant plucked out another hair.

"Ouch. Being beautiful hurts."

"Once all the fuss dies down about you accusing your uncle in the temple, Mother plans a big party to welcome her 'second daughter.' We will have fine food and wine, and Mother will hire a harper from Thebes. We haven't had a party like that since Father went away."

"Do you miss him? Ouch!" Maïa pushed away the servant. "Enough! If I am any more beautiful, the sun-god himself will be jealous!"

"Ha! Yes, I miss my father. When he is home, Mother is always in a good mood and never snaps at me. She has snapped a lot ever since my sister died."

In a low voice Maïa said, "You are lucky to have a father. Mine died, burned up by a fever. . . ."

"Like my sister!" Meret gripped her wrist.

Maïa nodded. "Watch — this is the abbreviated sign for weeping. It is all right to make it this way, together." She traced the eye shape and dotted the tears flowing down.

Meret copied the sign in the air, and somehow, as they made the sorrow drops, the eye became a shared eye, and the tears, their common tears.

Well before dawn the next day, Maïa sneaked down to the kitchen, carrying a fresh shift and sandals to wear to the trial. Teti was not yet up, firing the oven in the yard. Along one wall of the kitchen were large clay storage jars and yesterday's bread was in a net bag against the wall.

Maïa stood on tiptoe and took down two loaves of bread. She filled a flask with water from the jar, put both in a small carrying sack, and went down to where the narrow wooden skiff was tied to the floating dock. Depositing the bag of food and the clothes inside, Maïa climbed in, untied the boat, and pushed hard against the dock, sending the skiff out toward the current that would carry her north to Thebes.

Using the tall paddle, Maïa dug deep into the water. When the boat wobbled, Maïa breathed out a prayer: "Oh, let there be no hippos, Amun, let all crocodiles still sleep. . . ."

It was risky going to Thebes by boat, but the road was even more dangerous for young girls. Dangerous men might seize her and force her against her will. Maïa thought if she kept a steady pace she could reach Thebes before nightfall.

What would Nefert and Meret say when they found her gone? She could not tell Meret of her plans, for she would not have let her go. Maïa worried they would think her ungrateful and a thief. She paused, laying the paddle across the bow and turning to look back. In the dawn, she saw the dim outlines of Nefert's estate. By the house a light flared; Maïa thought it must be Teti starting the cooking fire.

She pressed her hand to the ache in her chest. She was leaving behind safety and people who protected her; ahead lay questions, uncertainty, and danger. But at the end of her journey she hoped to find Seti and hear him say, "Sister! Here you are at last!"

She remembered the dream where Mother gave her colored notes. "This is for bravery," she'd said of the purple one. Maïa imagined a purple note falling from the sky into her mouth, filling her with courage.

As the darkness lifted and the sky turned gray, Maïa took up her paddle and thrust the boat forward, past the flooded palms. If she kept farther away from shore, the current would help carry her north, and her arms would not tire so easily. Maïa pulled the paddle toward her — again and again. A heron called harshly from the reeds, and downriver a hippo bellowed. For a moment, Maïa rested her paddle and ate some bread, drinking from the water flask.

In the trees by shore, a flock of ibis shook out their wings. In the early light, they looked pearly, luminescent, like a collection of jewels on a god's throat. Something splashed nearby, and Maïa gripped her paddle, peering ahead. A long shape slid into the river, and a snout with two nostrils went across her path, heading toward the opposite shore. Maïa sighed and pushed the boat forward.

Once Aunt had told a horrible story about a crocodile that had eaten a whole family — father, mother, and little girl — seizing their legs and dragging them under the river to drown.

The son, who was the only one left, did not know where to leave his mortuary offerings for his family to help them live on in the land of the west. Even though he had never heard of anyone doing this, each day he walked sadly to the river and left a loaf of bread and a cup of wine, thinking, perhaps rightly, that offering to the living coffin of his family — the crocodile — was the best that he could do.

The sun rose and the river turned red. The rays touched the opposite bank of the Nile, lighting the red cliffs of the desert. Ahead, a fish broke the surface of the water. A bird called harshly from a thicket of green reeds on her right and, heart pounding, Maïa made the boat go faster, despite the ache in her arms. *O Amun, protect me this day. Let no toothed monster eat me. Let no hippo toss me into the river. Protect me, your daughter who found the thief.*

Something like courage flowed into her again — she could feel it, like a fresh sluice of water inside. Her eyes widened, and she smiled. The god was with her today; she would not be food for the crocodiles.

Chapter Fourteen

The sun had been up for some time, long enough to make the air feel like coals baking bread. Maïa thought if she shut her eyes and held her hand out, she could imagine herself crouched beside Ipi, hand seared by the fire.

Shouts echoed over the water from behind, and she turned, suddenly wary. A large boat came around a curve, water shining and dripping as countless oars lifted and dropped, lifted and dropped. A thickset man stood in the bow, scanning the river.

He hailed her. "Daughter, where are you going?"

"I am out fishing, Master." She held up the net.

"Ah, but are they about at this time of the day?"

"Fish are always about, Master." Maïa dipped the net into the water, pretending to search beneath the surface. The net suddenly felt heavier, as if a fish had swum right into it. Laughing, Maïa lifted it, thinking that luck was with her. But it was not a shining, silver shape in the middle but something brown and hideous.

Maïa cried out. "It's a hand — someone's hand!"

The man on the near boat looked down, cursed, then loudly chanted a prayer as the boat swept past. Maïa's fingers locked on the handle, and her breathing stuttered like a snared rabbit. She could neither let go of the net nor dump its horrible contents back into the Nile.

A hand! Like the ones Meret told me soldiers cut off in battle. But there are no battles here — more likely a crocodile. Amun, help my fingers to let go! May his ka *live forever.*

The boat swung sideways in the current, and with one final cry, Maïa threw the entire net into the water. She seized the paddle, driving the boat forward as the net sank from sight.

"Ugh, horrible, ugh!"

She tried not to look into the water, but a sudden movement caught her eye. A long green snout opened wide, grabbed the entire net, and dove under the surface. Its tail gave a great slap as it disappeared, rocking the skiff wildly from side to side.

Maïa paddled backward and thrust out to the side to steady the boat.

She eyed the water fearfully, aware that the crocodile could surface at any moment, even beneath her. She cried, "Amun, Bes, and Hathor protect me now!"

Then — as the ripples subsided and the boat steadied once more — she thought of the purple note from the dream. She imagined it floating above, coming down into her open mouth. Courage and bravery would come, if not now, then later.

After a time, she saw that the crocodile had gone away, and the only thing disturbing the water were other boats — smaller ones fishing, men calling out to one another, and larger ones laden with cargo. Most were going north to Thebes, but a few were sailing upriver, white sails stretched to catch the wind. She breathed deeply, her stomach still churning.

Now the sun was directly overhead, the river was thick with traffic, and Maïa had to keep her wits to avoid the bigger craft. From behind, she heard the hissing sound of a vessel moving through water. A long sloop came up along her left side, its rowers dipping their oars again and again. In the back stood a burly man, steering with a long wooden oar.

"Ho, Daughter!" he hailed her. "Fishing today?"

Maïa shook her head mutely; she was afraid she might vomit if she tried to speak. As the boat went past, it rocked from side to side in the current. Stacked on the deck were rows of large clay jars, all tightly sealed, probably going to the temple of Karnak.

Concentrating on the silver drops running off her paddle, Maïa struggled to erase the image of the severed hand. *Was it a man's?* The fingers had been thick and broad, like a workman's. A shuddering began inside, running up her toes, her legs, and seizing her middle. Her shoulders shook and teeth chattered, despite the blazing sun.

She would not get sick. To keep her fear at bay, Maïa remembered lying on the roof of her parents' home long ago. Mother would sing a song before they slept, as the stars shone overhead. Father would reach out to pat Mother's shoulder, then Maïa's, then Seti's, linking them all together with his touch.

The shuddering slowed, leaving a knotted stomach and a bitter taste at the back of her throat. She had to stop and drink from her flask, eat some bread. That would help her pounding head and aching arms.

Where could she stop? On her right, dense thickets of reeds stretched along the bank of the river; to her left, river traffic was thick and noisy. Paddling slowly, Maïa sent the boat into the outer edge of the reeds. A soft shushing surrounded her as the prow nosed through the tall sedges. Though the air was still and hot, there was some shade. Wedging the boat into the reeds, Maïa thought she could safely stay here a while.

Birds fluttered overhead, and a duck quonked nearby. After drinking deeply from the flask, Maïa tried a bite of bread. But it stuck in her throat. Eating was impossible. Maïa pulled her linen head-piece over her face, lay back, and closed her eyes.

But in the dark behind her eyelids the hand kept appearing, like a hieroglyph imprinted on papyrus. Sighing, she sat up but was startled by a sudden thump above. Something large and dark hurtled into the skiff, followed quickly by a second shape.

"*Aiee!*"

Maïa scrambled to the end of the boat, looking wildly about. Was it a crocodile? But the boat was still and did not rock. Then Maïa saw a duck with a broken neck and wings spread out. The sun shone on a patch of colorful blue feathers, and Maïa's breath slowed. The other object was a curved wooden hunting stick. *Not a hand, it is not a hand.*

"Hey there! You, girl! Have you seen my duck?"

A young man paddled his skiff through the reeds. "I thought I saw it fall just about here. . . ."

Shivering, Maïa held up the duck and the hunting stick. The words "Here they are" sounded garbled, as if spoken by a toothless old man.

As he brought his boat close enough to touch hers, he reached for the duck, taking it quickly with a proud look, and then the hunting stick. But before he turned his skiff, he took a closer look at Maïa's bowed head and shaking shoulders.

"What is wrong, girl? Are you ill?" He leaned away from her, eyes narrowed.

"No — not ill — I saw a cut-off hand in the water. . . . I caught it in my fishing net. . . ."

"Oh." Just one word, but it held sympathy, and it unlocked Maïa's mouth.

"I was fishing, you see, and my net caught this . . . thing . . . and I couldn't get it out so I threw it away . . . and I said a prayer for the *ka* . . ." Her words ran out, like the last drops from a water clock.

"Ah, Maiden, that is something to test one's courage. Of course" — he squared his shoulders — "I have seen many severed hands, in battle, for I am a soldier in Hatshepsut's army. I am called Khonsu."

He seemed to be awaiting her name, but she was afraid to give it. In fact, now that she thought of it, Maïa realized that this could be just the sort of person Nefert would want her to avoid on the road. Seizing her paddle, Maïa began to move toward the edge of the reeds.

"Wait, Maiden, I will not harm you! Would you like me to come with you wherever you are going? I do not think you should be on the river alone."

She looked back at him. His words were kind; even his face, despite the proud expression and hawk's eyes, did not look dangerous. If only she could see through the skin covering his chest, to see his heart's thoughts.

"Maiden, I will not harm you. I promise."

She was too raw, too queasy, her body too full of the ache of travel to resist. "Then" — she nodded — "I welcome your company."

Together, they moved their boats through the last of the reeds out onto the open river. Maïa's heart slowed, the inner shaking disappeared. Now she had company, and if a green snout crossed the river in front of her, she would not face it alone.

After paddling for a long time, with sweat running down her arms, face, and back, Maïa turned to Khonsu. "Have you been in Thebes lately?"

He nodded, driving the boat forward. "I live near Hatshepsut's palace."

"Have you . . ." She hesitated. "Have you any news of a trial at the temple of Karnak?"

He raised his eyebrows but said nothing.

"About a priest who took grain from the temple?"

"No, Maiden, I have not heard any news. That is a serious crime. The court could exile him, or cut off his —" Too late, he stopped.

Maïa bit her lips. "Cut off what?"

Khonsu shook his head slightly. "Sometimes the judgment is to cut off a person's ears, mouth, or nose, even a hand. Other times, it is exile — or death." He brought his skiff nearer to hers in silent sympathy, and together they went north, keeping away from the middle of the river where there were too many boats. The sun headed toward its home in the west, rays lighting fire on the tops of the red cliffs to her left. Maïa thought of Hatshepsut's mortuary temple there — of its beauty and the incense trees planted on the terrace (so Uncle had told her), brought all the way from the land of Punt.

She was thinking so hard about the temple that her boat knocked against Khonsu's.

"Maiden! Be careful. Usually, I stop near the palace, there." He gestured to a large dock, busy with boats and people coming and going. "But I would like to continue with you, if you wish it."

Maïa noticed the outlines of a sprawling white building, with palm trees in front and green land running down to a dock. The people and their friendly shouts were comforting, a sharp contrast to the task ahead. "I shall be all right. . . ." Suddenly, she shivered, remembering the severed hand and the green snout of the crocodile. "Though it is not far to my old home, Khonsu."

He grinned at her and kept paddling by her side. "Then I shall come with you."

Well, I did pray for safety on the way to Thebes, and this must be the answer, Maïa thought, glad that Khonsu had decided to stay with her. As they paddled downriver, the current pushing them slightly behind, she looked for the one landmark she thought she could recognize from the water, a lone palm tree that had been blasted in a thunderstorm. Its blackened fronds hung uselessly in the wind, making a dry rustling.

"What will you do when you reach your

destination — Maiden?" Khonsu looked over at her, wiping the sweat from his eyes with one hand.

"Maïa," she said. "My name is Maïa. I have something I must do. My brother, Seti, he is a scribe in the temple and needs my help."

"Ah, I have a sister who is much loved. She will be married soon, and lucky is the man who gets her."

Maïa frowned momentarily, remembering Aunt's harsh words about what man would want a girl who was never there when needed. They paddled on in silence, with Maïa looking intently at the shore. She saw two workers building a mud dike at the far edge of the fields. And nearby was the blasted palm tree, like something the god Seth would destroy in a storm.

"There! There is my landmark, Khonsu. This is where I stop, and I thank you. Your company has been a balm to me, after that horrid — horrid — thing. . . ." She could not say the word "hand."

"Then I will leave you, once you are ashore." They headed their skiffs to the flattened edge of the river, and Khonsu jumped into shallow water first. Tying his boat around a stump, he helped drag her skiff onto land.

"How long do you stay?" Khonsu stretched and

put his hands on the small of his back. The sun glinted on a gold ring on his right hand.

"As long as it takes me to help my brother." Her face was so dried by the sun it was hard to smile at Khonsu. Briefly, she touched his arm. "Thank you."

He smiled. "Remember my name. If you ever need my help, I am quartered near the palace." He turned, untied his skiff, and with a running jump, turned the boat and paddled back toward the palace.

Maïa watched him go, the last rays of the setting sun staining his boat bloodred. She shivered, hoping it was not a bad omen. Taking up her bag of food and her clothes, Maïa turned to walk across the fields to the lane that led home.

Chapter Fifteen

When she reached the lane, she passed an old man returning home, leaning heavily on a staff. "Evening, Maiden," he said, and she returned the greeting.

"Good health to you." The words faltered and stuck in her throat. Where could she go? Aunt's house was impossible, but how to get news of Seti?

Maïa paused in the road, and a thin dog with a scrappy tail raced past, a piece of bread in its mouth. A little boy followed, waving a stick and shouting, "Come back, thief!"

Thief. That is what they called Uncle. What was happening to him? Could she even find where the trial was so she could be a witness? She rubbed one bare foot against her leg. If she wanted news, the place to go was Mistress Hunro's house. The old woman sat outside much of the day, talking to passersby and gathering news. Maïa also knew that she could get water there. She had finished hers a long time ago, and her throat ached with thirst and weariness.

Maïa lifted her head, inhaling the air and smells of Thebes: dust, donkey dung, baking bread, a whiff of perfumed oil, and the hot breeze from the river. When she reached the small shrine to Hathor, Maïa laid some bread at her feet, saying a prayer for protection.

She walked up the lane that passed near her old house. There was the small mud-brick dwelling of Mistress Hunro. Washing was spread out to dry on some bushes in front. Maïa followed the thin sound of a woman singing behind the house.

"Mistress Hunro?" The old woman, with only a few strands of white hair on her head, sat in the shade of a tree, unknotting string in her lap.

"Yes, Daughter?" She peered at her, and Maïa realized she could not see her well enough to recognize her.

"It is Maïa. Maïa," she repeated, coming closer.

"Ah, we wondered what happened to you! Your

aunt is in a rage — so I have heard from the neighbors." She looked up at her, mouth pursed.

"Do you have any water?" Maïa crouched in the shade of the tree, panting. As she set down her sack, she felt like weeping. Everything seemed to collapse inside, like a child's stick house that falls to pieces in a hot wind. She could go no farther.

Mistress Hunro rose, went inside, and returned with a water flask. "Where have you come from, Maïa, to make you so tired and sweaty?"

Maïa drank and swallowed, drank and swallowed again until her thirst was quenched. "I found a friend, Mistress Hunro, who took me in, for I know I cannot go home to Aunt's. I am so worried about Seti, I miss him, and is he living with my aunt, how can I find out where the trial is . . . ?"

Mistress Hunro shushed her with one hand. "Be calm, Daughter. He still lives with your aunt, though I hear she has become strangely quiet. The trial is at the temple of Karnak. First, you must bathe and have some food." She motioned to a jug of water under the shade tree. "Wash with that while I find you something to wear."

Maïa stripped off her shift and upended the jar. Water ran over her hair, face, arms, and body, and she scrubbed as it dripped down. For a moment, she remembered Meret and the bath they shared her first day at Nefert's estate. What was her friend doing now? Was Meret worried or angry with her?

Maïa rubbed her face with her wet hands; she could not think about them now, not until she had found the trial and told the truth. Briefly, she touched the Maat feather inside her amulet bag: Her Majesty honored the truth, as did the gods.

Mistress Hunro returned, holding out a graying shift. "Wear this for now, it is clean. And in the meantime, tell me how you came to be in the temple of Luxor, asking questions of the god." Her eyes gleamed as she led Maïa into the house.

Maïa sat on the floor mat, eating lentils and bread and drinking barley beer as she told her old neighbor all that had happened.

At the end of her tale, Mistress Hunro grasped Maïa's arm in a surprisingly strong clasp. "Be careful, Maïa. Remember that whatever judgment they make on your uncle will also fall on you, Seti, and your aunt. The priests of Amun will not forget that you brought shame on them."

Would Paneb remember her? Maïa wondered. The fleshy face with its odd, naked eyes rose up in her mind — he had not forgotten. But even worse was her fear that Seti was still angry with her for exposing Uncle's theft. If he could only hear her story, he would not be angry.

Holding a flickering oil lamp, Mistress Hunro beckoned Maïa to follow her up the ladder to the roof. With small contented sounds, the older woman settled on her sleeping mat, patting one for Maïa.

"Tomorrow you can go to the temple, where the trial is, and be a witness. Sleep well this night." Mistress Hunro blew out the lamp, and darkness closed around them.

So many nights Maïa had spent like this at Uncle's house. It seemed flood-seasons away, as if that girl were someone else with a different face, different dreams, afraid of other, lesser things.

Mistress Hunro sent her off the next morning with a flask of water, and many instructions to keep safe. "Remember, tell the guards you are there for the trial. Tell them that you are an important witness."

Maïa looked over her shoulder at her older neighbor. "Do not worry. Someday soon I will come back and give you all the news."

"Thank you, Daughter!" Mistress Hunro raised one hand in what looked like a blessing.

Turning, Maïa walked along the way that led to the temple of Karnak. Though she was dressed in her clean linen shift, with hair combed and sandals on, she was not ready for what was ahead.

Everything seemed so ordinary. There was a woman carrying a great pile of baskets to market, stacked so high on her head that it seemed impossible. Maïa passed an old man with a staff who asked where she was hurrying to. A boy chased a girl down the street, only to stop at the outraged yells of a man carrying a platter of honey cakes.

Though her legs and arms were sore from her river journey, Maïa forced herself to walk swiftly. When the morning was still fresh, she reached the stone-paved road leading to the temple. She faltered as she looked at the white stone buildings shining in the blazing light.

Remember the purple song note from your mother — it will give you courage. You are Maïa of Thebes, almost a scribe, and a witness. Courage! she told herself.

Soldiers stood guard outside the temple, looking fierce with bows slung over their shoulders and clubs at their sides. Maïa paused, rubbing one foot against her left leg. Was it safe to go inside? Priest Paneb was sure to be there; she had not forgotten his malevolent words on the day of the accusation.

She made herself walk forward. One soldier stepped up, barring her way. "Who are you, Maiden, to enter the temple while a trial is being held?" He held the tall, curved bow in front of her.

"I am Maïa of Thebes," she said softly, and he made to dismiss her.

"Off with you now, this is no place for you. Off!" Scowling, he shook his bow at her.

"But I am . . ."

"You are of no importance here, Maiden. Go!"

Suddenly, she stood straighter. "They are asking for me inside, and the priests will be angry if you keep me here. I am the niece of the priest Hay who is on trial."

The guard stepped backward, coughed, and said, "Ah, that is different. You are not a nobody. You are kin to a thief!"

Keeping silent, Maïa stepped through the doorway into the dim light of the temple. Inside, the air smelled of stale incense. A narrow beam of light lay across the stone floor, leading up to a table where men in priests' garb sat on stools. Standing before them was a shrunken figure, like something left too long in the sun and wind.

It was Uncle Hay, with a bent head, and to his left stood Seti and Aunt Nebet, dressed in their finest clothes and anointed with scented oils, as if that would somehow aid Uncle's cause.

"Maïa!" Seti held out his arms. "You have come to help!" She wanted to run over and embrace him, but she faltered at the sight of the man at the head of the table. It was Paneb, dressed in a white linen kilt, wearing a gold amulet, and with a fine wig on. Only his strange eyes moved, widening at the sight of her, then narrowing to slits.

Maïa took a deep breath and stepped forward. "I am here — Maïa, niece of the priest Hay."

Seti moved toward her but was stopped by a fierce look from Aunt. She kept her head turned away from Maïa. But Uncle hobbled up, saying with a strange grimace, "Thank Amun you are here, my dear niece. You will tell the priests what they wish to know. . . ." *That I am not guilty*, his eyes pleaded.

Paneb stared at her, his thick fingers resting on the table. "Now is your chance to tell what happened, girl, to put things right."

Maïa paused, uncertain. She knew that Paneb wished her ill, but would the other priests believe her story? They represented the majesty and honor of the temple and its gods.

An older man with a golden ring looked up. "Paneb, I would like to question this witness. She is the niece of priest Hay, is that correct?"

At a nod from Paneb, the man began to question Maïa. "Daughter, your uncle is accused of a terrible crime, of stealing temple grain. You have accused him." He tapped his ringed finger on the table.

The musty air felt heavy, as if she had to struggle to push words out of her mouth. "Yes, I did."

"I would like to know how you came to suspect your uncle, a man of known integrity, who always follows the temple rules to the last detail. No one is more careful about purification!" The priests nodded their heads and looked angrily at Maïa.

"I — that is — sirs . . ." Maïa felt Seti's eyes on her and turned to see him with raised eyebrows, hands held out. He wanted her to lie. To save the family honor. To save Uncle Hay, even Aunt Nebet.

"But, sirs, first tell me the punishment for stealing grain from the temple."

"Well, I do not see why I cannot tell you. It is either . . ."

There was a sudden commotion at the doorway, and all heads turned to see an elegant woman dressed in the height of fashion with a wig on and a sparkling gold-and-blue pectoral adorning her chest. Beside her was a girl, equally fine.

"Meret! Nefert!" Maïa started to go to them, but Nefert waved her back.

"Please continue, honored priests. I have an interest in the proceedings as I am this girl's guardian. I am here to make certain she comes to no harm."

"Harm? Harm?" The word ran around the circle of seated men, and they recoiled. "No harm shall come to her here in the temple, Mistress!"

"I know all about the temple." Each word was sharp and solid as a fist on the table. "And its priests," she finished with a dark look at each man.

"Ahem. Let us proceed," continued the one who had been questioning Maïa. "Tell us how you suspected that the priest Hay was stealing temple grain."

"A suspicion only," Paneb inserted. "Only a suspicion, never proved."

"Not proved?" Maïa said, gathering courage. "Did you go to my uncle's house and look in the cellar?"

A wave of strong, intense feeling assailed Maïa, as if a cobra had risen up before her with its hood flared. It was the opposite of the feeling she'd had days before in the temple, when it seemed Amun was inside her like shimmering light.

Uncle Hay gave a piteous moan. "Niece, you know not what you saw. It was merely grain I bought from a neighbor, for I feared the harvest would be poor this year. You know we measure the flood height each year, and it seems it will be lower this time, so I was providing for my family, for you."

He was entirely different from the man she had once lived with, Maïa thought: diminished, shrunken, purged of his pride and arrogance.

"Tell them, Maïa," Nefert urged. "Tell them the truth."

Maïa fingered the golden Maat feather inside her amulet bag — her reward from Her Majesty for telling the truth. She must witness to what she had seen, and yet, if she did, what would happen to them?

The priest who had been questioning her stood. "In answer to your earlier question, Daughter, there are several punishments for stealing temple grain:

mutilation of the body, death, being thrown to the crocodiles, or exile."

At the word "exile" someone moaned to Maïa's left. When she turned, it was to see Aunt Nebet holding out her hands. "Not exile, honored priests, not that! To be buried in a foreign land is the final death!"

Maïa looked wildly around the table. "Sirs . . ." There was not a shred of compassion or kindness on any man's face. On her right side, Nefert challenged her with a fierce, compelling gaze. Only Meret smiled, placing her hand over her heart.

"Sirs . . ."

Seti caught her attention, inscribing something low beside his leg — it was a sign for weeping, an eye, with the dotted tears falling. She remembered how they had cried together when their parents died, how they had wept those first nights sleeping on the roof at Uncle's house. They had shared tears — they were brother and sister, kin, born from the same body. If she told the truth, he could be exiled, too, or punished in some terrible way. Mistress Hunro said that the family of a criminal shared in the judgment. It had never struck her before that *she* might be under sentence as well.

Maïa hung her head and muttered, "Sirs, I believed my uncle was taking grain from the temple, yet I have no proof. There is no proof," she said in a stronger voice.

Nefert cried out, "The clay seal that you found and the god's barque dipping forward in answer to your question — those are not proof? Amun himself answered her. You were there!"

Paneb smiled slightly and touched his amulet. "It has happened before that we have interpreted the god's words differently."

The older man with the gold ring rose and stared at Paneb. "Yet I say the god's word is to be trusted!"

A low sound swept around the room as different people voiced their opinions. Some challenged Paneb with the phrase, "The god's answer." Maïa felt faint and queasy; she had lied. In a place sacred to the gods, she had not told the whole truth.

Paneb thumped his hand down on the table. "We can pass judgment now. There is no proof that would call for mutilation or being thrown to the crocodiles, but my brother priests say we must honor the god's answer. Thus I say that the priest Hay and Lady Nebet shall be exiled to one of the oases where he can serve in a temple." The other priests chorused, "Yes, that must be so! That satisfies Maat."

A loud wail erupted, and Aunt Nebet sank to the floor, weeping. "I beg of you — not exile! Or — if exile — let us return to be buried in Egyptian soil!"

As no one would promise her that, the wails continued. Maïa sagged with relief. At least Uncle would not have his hand, mouth, ears, or nose cut off; she would not have to bear the guilt of that forever. To her right came a long sigh of disappointment and the sound of a foot stamped impatiently on the floor. Maïa did not dare look at Nefert.

"And what of my brother, sirs?" Maïa asked.

"What of who, Daughter?" Paneb said. It was hard to hear over Aunt's moaning.

"My brother, Seti, who is studying in The House of Life here at this very temple. Is he to be punished as well? He knew nothing of this."

Paneb turned to look at Seti. "I say the boy should stay here, for we have need of him. Scribes are too valuable to waste even one."

Seti's face broke into a grin, as he ran forward to hug Maïa. "Sister, oh, Sister, I have missed you!" For her ear alone he whispered, "Thank you!"

The wailing stopped as Aunt Nebet got to her

feet, wiping her eyes on her dress sleeve. She came up to Maïa and gripped her shoulder. "I do not thank you, Niece. It was an evil day when I took you into my house. Look how you have repaid us."

But Uncle Hay had a different response. He touched her briefly before leaving with the soldiers, holding his hand out into the shaft of sunlight. They both knew what he said silently, how his hand thanked her for her mercy.

Chapter Sixteen

Nefert put a hand on her arm and sighed. "I wish that you had . . ."

Meret started to chatter, "So exciting . . . Maïa . . . and this is your brother, Seti. . . ."

Maïa let Seti put his arms around her, listened to his whispered thanks, and tried to hug him back. She put one finger on the crescent moon mark on his shoulder, loving it and loving him. Yet she felt as if she were paddling down the Nile, and that a great boat had passed, tossing her in its wake.

They all were part of a tight group of people, talking at once, when suddenly Maïa felt the room darken. Paneb was standing in front of her, with the two soldiers from outside.

"You, girl, nuisance, you are *not* free to go. You will be punished with your family. That is the law."

Maïa gaped at him, and Nefert intervened. "What do you mean she is not free to go? She came here and testified — not telling the entire truth" — the woman bared her teeth at the priest — "and she is under my protection. I am Lady Nefert, and my husband, Mekhu, is a commander at the southern garrison. Her Majesty favors him," she added.

"It matters not," Paneb declared. "This girl is under the judgment of the priests of Karnak! She is coming with me."

Seti grabbed Maïa's arm. "Sir, please! You are gracious to me, be the same to my sister. She is innocent, and my sister can write."

Paneb did not bother to answer, but only nodded to the soldiers to proceed. They closed on either side, marching Maïa off through the outer door. Dimly, she was aware of her brother leaping and running beside her, shouting, "Sir, please, my lord!" She heard Nefert's protest, "You have no right!" then her command, "Find Pashed!"

In a moment they were outside. The sun hit her eyes, and Maïa was momentarily blinded. The entire world was burned white, colorless, and Maïa was certain of only one thing — she was a prisoner. Cloaked in the law, the wrath of Paneb had snared her at last.

"Where are you taking me?" Maïa stumbled at the fast pace of the soldiers. Paneb was right behind her; she could feel him walking heavily, breathing, and sending out a body heat that felt like hatred.

"To a safe place," he answered.

Maïa saw she was being hustled behind the temple down a side street. Paneb hurried in front, leading them to the end of the lane, past a series of mud-brick houses, across a street, until they finally reached a jumble of buildings in an unknown part of the city. When she turned, she thought she saw a tall shadow at the end of the street.

One soldier went up to the door of a dusty brown building and knocked. A man with a drooping eyelid poked his head out. "What do you want?" he asked roughly.

"We have brought a prisoner, the niece of a thief, and the priest Paneb says she must be locked up."

Paneb coughed and adjusted his wig. "This is the end of your journey, at the prison of Thebes. It is where you deserve to be — you . . ." He brought his fleshy face close, and the beads of sweat on his upper lip gleamed in the light. ". . . You traitor, bringer of dishonor to the sacred temples and their glorious priests!"

His strong scent assailed Maïa, and she cringed as he barked, "Take her away. Do not let her out." Then he strode out of sight, the soldiers following.

Maïa did not move until the man with the drooping eyelid struck her arm. "Get moving, girl. I will not stand here all day!" She yelped and jerked forward.

Nudging her with the stick, and occasionally hitting her arm, back, or shoulder, the jailer moved her through the chamber, up a set of stairs, and down a dark corridor that smelled of urine. He opened a door to a small room and pointed to a thin mat on the floor — "your bed" — and to a clay pot in the corner — "and where you relieve yourself. I will not have a stinking room, girl, so watch out!"

Maïa swayed as the jailer closed and bolted the door behind her. She was locked in a coffinlike room barely longer than she was tall. One high window showed a patch of light, but no breeze came through it. The walls were a rough brown with scrape marks down the sides. From former prisoners? Maïa had a terrible image of a man clawing his nails down the walls, praying for release. She began to breathe in quick short breaths. Red and green spots appeared before her eyes, and she fell to the mat.

She was in jail! She had heard about it from Uncle — a place of thieves and criminals. People died here. Pulling her knees as close as she could, Maïa rocked back and forth, back and forth.

Sweat dripped down Maïa's face, onto her chin, and dropped to the thin mat that was her bed. Through the high window all she could see was sky. A cloud passed by, shining red in the setting sun. She watched the sky change from red, to pink, to a faint blue. Then the window square turned dark, but no breeze made its way inside.

Footsteps sounded outside. She jumped up as someone fumbled with the bolt on the door; a thin young man set a plate of cucumbers and bread on the floor. Beside them he put a flask of water, looking at her out of the corners of his eyes. A scar ran down the right side of his face, and his shoulders were ridged with scars, as if from beatings that had healed badly.

"And what have you done, Maiden, to be in this jail?" He shook his head at her.

"I . . . I . . . ." Maïa opened her mouth but no words came out. Seizing the flask, she tipped it up and swallowed, again and again.

"I discovered my uncle was stealing grain from the temple," she explained wearily. "And I asked the question of Amun at the great ceremony, and he said that it was true."

"Ah, that is bad. You made the priests angry." It was not a question.

"Yes, I did, and my aunt and uncle are to be exiled. I was afraid they might cut off his nose or ears, and I thought exile would be better than that. But," she said, slumping onto the mat, "I was wrong."

The servant waved his hand at her, urging her to eat. "Listen to your dreams this night, Maiden. Perhaps they will tell you of your fate. I wish you were not here, but a priest is a dangerous enemy — and," he added in a whisper, "so is the head jailer."

He turned and locked the door after him.

Maïa forced herself to eat the cucumbers and bread, and to drink most of the water. She would save some for during the night. Stretching out her legs, she touched the pleats of the fine linen dress, a gift from Nefert.

Two days ago I was living on an estate with servants and friends, sleeping in a bed with a headrest, and eating fine foods. Now I am in jail like a common thief.

She wondered if the god Seth had had a hand in her dismal fate. Had she angered him? He was the author of storms and evil, chaos and shipwreck. And he had murdered his brother god, Osiris, cut him into pieces and scattered them far and wide. Only Osiris's sister-wife, Isis, had been able to find all the pieces and put him back together again.

Maïa felt as if she had been chopped into fragments and scattered over the earth. Who could find each one to fit them together into Maïa of Thebes?

Chapter Seventeen

She was sporting in the water, silver drops splashing around her. A fish leaped into the air, then plunged into the river. There was no danger anywhere — no crocodiles, no hippos — just water, green reeds, and her slim body swimming in the Nile.

She woke to find herself curled in a knot on the prison mat. The high window showed a square of clear dawn sky. One last star shone. It had been a good dream, not an evil one, for swimming in the river was a fine omen, according to Aunt.

Maybe Nefert could get her out of jail? Maybe that was Pashed, her servant, who had followed her yesterday to this place of shame?

Maïa plucked at her dress. It was crinkled and

stiff with sweat. Her last bath at Mistress Hunro's house seemed months ago, and she had not even had any salt paste to wash with. She smelled.

Maïa reached for the water and emptied it into her mouth, swishing it around to cleanse it. Then she stripped off her shift, shook it vigorously, and put it on again. She used the pot in the corner of the room, then waited for the servant to appear with food. That is, *if* he brought food in the morning.

The sounds and smells of the prison swelled around her. Though Maïa had been careful to use the pot, everything smelled of urine, sweat, and something indefinable — sour and desperate.

A man beat rhythmically against a wall, shouting at the same time. The words blurred together, but they reminded Maïa of a trapped animal. There was an answering shout, the sound of running feet, and the knocking on the wall stopped.

She jumped up and paced around the tiny room, holding her hands tightly together. She pretended that Mother was holding her hand, watching over her. Maïa sank down, closed her eyes, and remembered how Mother had sailed small reed boats on the reflecting pool at their old house; how, laughing, she had sent them off to the far side of the pool.

When the square of sky had burned to a brighter blue, someone unbolted her door and pulled it open. The young man set down another plate of cucumbers and bread, along with a flask of fresh water.

"Thank you." Maïa took up the food, squatting on her heels to eat. "I wish I had something else to eat besides cucumbers, not that I am not grateful. . . ."

"For such a pretty maiden as you, I wish you had roasted duck and a cup of wine." He cocked his head, giving her a sharp look.

Maïa noticed his shoulder bones sticking out and his bowed legs. One of the welts on his shoulder ran all the way down to his wrist. "How did you get that?"

He jerked his head in the direction of the stairway, and Maïa knew it was the head jailer's work.

"He has hurt us both." Maïa cradled the water flask.

"That is what he does, especially when he drinks —" At the sound of feet on the stairs, he hurriedly closed the door and bolted it. "Later," he hissed.

"Wait, come back. Do not leave me here alone. . . . Tell me your name." Maïa jumped up and hit the wooden panel.

"Petara," came through the door. "Hush!"

Maïa could not stop beating her fists against the wood. The panic that she had kept at bay rose inside. She was in a coffin — there was no air to breathe — she would starve and her bones would poke out of her skin like sticks — her *ka* would wander wailing and then be quenched into nothingness like a blown-out lamp. . . .

"Stop that noise!" A harsh voice barked.

The door crashed open and standing in its frame was the rough guard from yesterday. He raised a stout stick and brought it down hard on her shoulder. She cringed, scurrying back to the end of the room. But it was not far enough.

He came inside, crashing the stick from side to side and growling out threats. "I have the power to hurt you — that priest said not to hold back — see what we do to prisoners. . . ." Grabbing her left hand, he brought the stick down on her open palm.

"*Aiee!*" Tears ran down into her mouth, and the jailer grinned. His broken, blackened teeth frightened Maïa so much that she stopped crying immediately.

Holding her wounded hand, Maïa pressed her body against the wall. He grinned again at her attempts to escape, and Maïa made herself stay still. Gathering her courage as if it were a rope in her hands, she said, "You have no right to beat me. I am Maïa of Thebes, and I have important friends at the palace. . . ."

"I do not care who you know!" He thumped the stick on the floor, making Maïa jump. "You are *my* prisoner, and I have orders to keep you safe and tight in this room. This is how we treat scum!" He struck her other shoulder.

She yelped with pain, but Maïa made herself stare back, daring him to hit her again. And as she stared, she prayed inside to the one who had always protected her: *Amun, stay his hand! Punish him! Make his bowels turn to water! Let his eye never stop weeping! Please help me.*

Praying with her eyes wide open, Maïa stretched out her wounded hand, willing all the pain and hurt inside to flow into him.

The man moved away from her. His eyelids fluttered, and his hand opened and closed on the club. "You — do not look at me like that — this is a spell, I see. . . ." He backed out of the door and slammed it shut, muttering charms as he bolted it.

Now what had she done? He would think her dangerous and might punish her even more. But it was the only way to stop the beating. Maïa sank onto the mat, cradling her left hand in her lap. It was useless, fingers turning inward like a claw. And her shoulders? They burned from the club, and her skin was already turning purple.

For a moment she thought of Hathor, how she brought joy, beauty, and music to their lives. But when she was angered, she turned from a gentle goddess into a devouring lioness — Sekhmet. *Come to my aid now. Punish this cruel jailer as he deserves!*

"Mother," she whispered, crying now. "Mother."

When the window framed a black sky, the door opened cautiously, and the servant stuck his head in. Maïa sat on the mat, keeping very still.

"Maiden? Are you all right? Sennefer is drinking wine with his cronies, and I take this chance to talk with you. Be careful! Be quiet, if you value your life!" He set down a plate of lentils, bread, and a small cup of barley beer.

"Oh, thank you, Petara, thank you!" She could not reach out for the food.

"What did he do to you?" Petara came closer.

Maïa lifted her arms, one hand clawed shut.

"The beast, demon, son of a stinking baboon . . ." He knelt before Maïa, taking up some bread and putting it gently into her mouth. "He would not treat a dog this way!"

Maïa chewed and swallowed, and chewed and swallowed until the lentils and bread were gone. Then Petara tipped the flask of barley beer to her lips, and Maïa drank greedily, some dribbling down her chin.

"My only bath this day," she whispered. "Would you help me?"

He got up from the floor and gathered the flask. "I can do nothing, Maiden. I am just a servant with an evil master."

"Please." Wincing as she stood, Maïa reached inside her amulet bag with her right hand and took out the gold Maat feather. "Take this to the palace. Tell them I am imprisoned here — Maïa of Thebes. If you meet Her Majesty's soldiers, ask for Khonsu. He is my friend and will help me. Please!"

He eyed her, then rubbed his nose vigorously. "I cannot, Maiden. If I am found out, the master would beat me until I bled — again."

"Do you not have a sister — like me? Would you not want someone to help her? I did nothing wrong, except to anger a powerful priest."

As he still hesitated, Maïa said, "We are both prisoners. Quick, bring me a burnt stick from the fire. If I write a message, will you take it to the palace?"

"*You* write?" His eyebrows shot up. "A girl?"

Maïa was so hurt that her lips ached. "I will help you — if you help me."

Staring at her for a moment, Petara grimaced, then bowed his head. "All right, I will do what you ask, but promise to reward me if you are freed."

"Of course . . . I give you my oath."

He took the gold feather from her and tucked it into his own amulet bag. "I promise to deliver this to the palace and to give them your name. Maïa of Thebes?"

She nodded and watched as he shut the door, bolting it behind him. In a short while, he returned, holding out a blackened stick. "This is all I could find, but we are lucky — Sennefer is still drinking wine. Hurry!"

Kneeling, Maïa told Petara to tear a piece of linen from the bottom of her shift; she could not do it herself. Luckily, her right hand was unhurt, and with the burnt stick she wrote the symbols for "Maïa" on the fabric, then the hieroglyphs for *djedeni em maat,* "I have spoken in truth."

In the temple when Maïa told Hatshepsut about her uncle's thievery, she had used those very words: "I have spoken in truth." Her Majesty *must* remember her.

Maïa rolled the fabric up, handing it to Petara. Sweating with fear, he thrust it deep inside the top band of his loincloth. Without another word, he left, and Maïa heard his hurried footsteps going downstairs.

In the night sky a star came out, then another. They shone down on her as they also shed light on her friends — Nefert, Meret, Ipi, and Seti. Were they trying to free her or did they not have the power to do so? But the feather and her message to Hatshepsut — they would have to work. They *had* to.

CHAPTER EIGHTEEN

Maïa woke to the sound of a bolt being drawn back. Jumping to her feet, she cried out at the pain in her shoulders and hand — still useless at her side. The window showed a faint square of pink; it was dawn.

The door swung back, and Petara stuck his head inside. "Maïa? I went to the palace and gave the gold feather and your written name to that soldier —"

"Khonsu!"

"That one. But hush! I hear someone on the stairs. . . ." He withdrew his head, and Maïa heard the sound of raised voices outside.

A woman snapped, "I am her guardian with a letter from Hatshepsut!"

Then came the sound of a scuffle, something hitting the wall, and Khonsu's raised voice. "Open that door immediately!"

The door swung back, and Khonsu burst into the room, followed closely by Nefert.

"Oh, my daughter, what did they do to you?" Nefert took her in her arms, laying Maïa's head on her shoulder.

Maïa burst into tears. She was finally safe and, as she wept, Khonsu gathered her sandals from the mat and went to the door. "We must leave — now."

Sennefer hovered outside, club raised. "You have no right to take my prisoner."

"Hatshepsut herself gives us that right — jailer!" Nefert waved a papyrus in his face, showing him the hieroglyphs inside the two cartouches. Even he recognized his ruler's name and drew back with a frightened expression.

Khonsu strode past him, and pressed the jailer against the wall until he fell to the floor, breathless. Khonsu then trod on him, saying, "Oh, excuse me, is this a piece of monkey dung in the corridor? Someone should clean it up!"

At the head of the stairs, Petara waited, grinning with delight at Sennefer coiled on the floor.

"I thank you, Slave. . . ." Nefert said to the young man, who protested, "Servant, Mistress, not slave. And remember your promise, Maïa."

Leaning against Nefert, Maïa said, "I promised I would help him."

"And so we shall. Hurry, you are coming with us."

Before Sennefer could rise and protest, they hurried downstairs, through the door, and out into the street where two carrying chairs awaited. Gently, Khonsu helped Maïa into one and told the two bearers they were going to the palace. Nefert climbed into the other, and off they went at a trot, with Khonsu and Petara close behind.

"Mistress, what are your plans for me?" Petara walked swiftly beside Nefert's carrying chair.

"You protected my second daughter, and I am sure we can find a place for a good servant." She glanced at the scars on his arm. "No one is ever beaten in my house!"

"My mistress, I can take care of cloth, I know how to clean all things in a household, I can cook, braid rushes into sandals, even make papyrus scrolls — I think."

They hurried to put the stinking alley behind them, the bearers traveling toward the palace road.

Maïa's head was swimming, and her stomach felt hollow and empty.

"We will be there soon, Maïa," Nefert called. "Are you all right? Sometimes when prisoners are freed, their wits have gone swimming with the crocodiles." Nefert looked at her with a sudden, wounded expression. The edges of her mouth trembled.

"I am all right, my second mother," Maïa called back, and saw Nefert's face open like a flower.

Soon the bearers left the main road and headed on to a stone lane. Trees arched overhead, shading the way, and the breeze smelled fresh. Maïa saw the white lines of the sprawling palace, with the Nile sparkling just beyond.

Near a side door, the bearers set down the two chairs. Nefert stepped out and extended a hand to Maïa, but Khonsu was already lifting her out.

"I fear I do not smell very good," she said in a small voice.

"That does not matter. You will have a bath inside the palace, get some ointment on those bruises, and I will see you later."

"Pashed?" Nefert called to her servant. "Please see that Petara — from the jail — is bathed and gets some fresh clothes."

A servant came and led them through a series of rooms with red and blue painted tiles on the floor. The walls were covered with bright decorations, and the columns were carved to look like tall stalks of papyrus. They went deeper into the palace until the servant stopped at a chamber with painted ducks flying above tall green reeds. Two beds with carved black headrests were in the center, and on one sat . . .

"Meret!" Maïa ran forward. "Oh, Meret." She collapsed onto the bed.

"There, there." Meret patted her lower back, away from the red welts on her shoulders. "That jail — what they did to you!"

Nefert stood close beside the bed. "Maïa, I tried to free you a day earlier, but I could not see Hatshepsut. But your scribbled letter and the Maat feather did the trick. Oh, my poor daughter! Eat before you bathe and go to Her Majesty."

On a table was a plate of warm bread, dates, and a cup of wine. Maïa devoured them all and asked, "Do you know where Seti is? Is he safe?"

"Yes, he is safe, Daughter. I brought him to the palace yesterday, and I think Her Majesty has plans for him."

Before Maïa could even wonder at that, a slight girl limped into the room, holding out her hands.

"Maïa!"

"Ipi! Oh, Ipi! How did they find you?"

Nefert smiled. "We discovered her at your uncle's house, alone since your uncle and aunt are being exiled. Meret told me all about her battle with the crocodile, and we need servants like her."

Ipi rushed over to Maïa, inspecting her shoulders and touching her injured hand. "What happened? No, do not tell me. Come with me."

Maïa followed Ipi to a nearby room paved with stones. "This is paradise — tell me I am not dead."

"You are not dead! Tush, tush, let me take off this filthy dress." Ipi raised one of the water jugs and poured it over Maïa's head. With a soft linen cloth dipped into a salt and water paste, Ipi rubbed Maïa's arms and legs, avoiding all the sore spots. After she was dry, Ipi put healing ointment on her welts. "What did they do to you in that jail?"

Maïa reveled in the sight of her old friend who had seen her through so many battles. Suddenly, she did not want to tell of her misery except to say, "I was seized by a human crocodile."

"Indeed, you were." They walked back to the room where Meret was waiting.

"Is Ipi coming home with us?" Maïa asked.

Ipi put her hands on her hips. "And why would I leave this fine new mistress — such an improvement over Lady Nebet with her complaints and worries about bad dreams!" Ipi held out a clean white dress with a beautiful green-and-red design coiling around its hem. "There — once we put on some makeup, you will be fit to meet Her Majesty."

Meret gestured at a young girl waiting near a small table. "Let the servant put on some eye makeup, and you will look better."

Maïa sat on a stool while the girl took out some pots from the cosmetic box. She combed Maïa's hair, anointing it with scented oil. With a small ivory stick, the servant carefully drew a green line around Maïa's eyes, coloring the top lid gray.

"You are ready, friend." Meret touched her hair lightly.

"Am I?" Maïa was not sure she was ready to be in the presence of the Lady of Two Lands, the Golden Horus, King of Upper and Lower Egypt, Daughter of Re. Fresh from prison, how could she meet with the divine daughter of a god?

CHAPTER NINETEEN

"I am afraid," Maïa whispered to Nefert as they walked along the corridor.

"My daughter, you know how to behave. There is nothing to fear."

They slowed before two tall carved doors. The copper framework around them was incised with hieroglyphs. "For Life, Prosperity, and Health, Forever, to Eternity," Maïa read aloud.

With her friends on each side, Maïa walked forward, across painted tiles that stretched to the far side of the room. If she looked only at her feet, Maïa thought she might be able to walk that vast distance to Her Majesty. First were the bright tiles and her sandaled feet passing from one to the next. To her side were soldiers in white leather helmets, standing straight and tall. Her sandals made a slight shushing sound, and it was hard to get her breath. Raising her eyes, Maïa saw a gilded throne on a raised dais, and sitting on it was the divine one of Amun, Hatshepsut, ruler of all.

Slight, with an oval face and intelligent eyes, she wore the golden cobra headpiece, a fine linen shift, and a pectoral of turquoise, red carnelian, and blue lapis lazuli. Afraid, Maïa looked only at the base of the throne. Hatshepsut's rouged feet were little in their red leather sandals. Even her feet looked divine, holy.

Aware that Nefert and Meret had let go of her arms, Maïa prostrated herself beside them on the floor. They did not stand until Hatshepsut commanded, "Rise, Maïa of Thebes, My Majesty welcomes you and your friends to the palace. My Majesty is pleased that you had the presence of mind to send the gold Maat feather to me and to write that message on the piece of cloth. Not many of us know how to write these days." She smiled slightly. "You showed initiative and courage, and that pleases me."

Maïa dared to lift her head and look at Her Majesty. Her eyes were lively, almost humorous, and there was not a trace of cruelty in her face.

"I think there is one more thing you wish from us, Maïa, is there not?"

"Your Majesty, the only thing I wish is for my brother, Seti, to be allowed to continue in The House of Life as a scribe. He is the one who taught me how to write, and he is my only brother."

Nefert touched her arm softly, as if to say, "That is enough, do not chatter on!"

"So he shall! Hapuseneb?" She turned to her counselor beside her. "Please bring the brother to me."

In a moment Seti was there, prostrating himself, then rising at Hatshepsut's command. Maïa did not dare turn and smile at him.

"Your brother shall remain in the temple if he so wishes, or he can return with Mistress Nefert."

"I wish . . ." Seti began, then faltered. He cleared his throat. "If Your Majesty wills it, I would stay in the temple and finish my studies."

"It shall be so." She nodded to them, and Maïa realized their audience was over; Hatshepsut's thoughts had already left them. Justice, Maat, had been done, and these small Egyptian lives would continue elsewhere.

"Wait — Hapuseneb," Her Majesty said. "The feather, please."

The counselor came down from the dais and placed the gold Maat sign in Maïa's right hand. He gave her one direct look from his dark eyes, and Maïa thought she saw respect there. Tucking the gold feather in her amulet bag, she bowed her head and backed out of the room, Seti and her friends beside her. Once through the doors, she turned and hugged her brother. "Here you are, at last!"

"Here I am. Now I can stop making the sign for weeping." Together, they traced the hieroglyph for an eye with tears falling from it.

"Stop it!" Nefert said. "No more signs in the air, especially in this palace! Come with me outside."

"Seti." Maïa squeezed his hand with her one good one. "I wish you were coming with us. I will miss you!"

"And I, you. But we can visit — Lady Nefert told me we could — and she said she is happy to have a second daughter who is also a scribe."

Maïa smiled. *A scribe.* She could hold that word in her hand, like the golden Maat feather. It would give her good luck and happiness, she knew it.

Following Nefert, they went through another

room until they saw an open doorway leading to a shaded garden. Light glanced off a reflecting pool with a blue lotus. Scattered bright cushions were set out under the trees, and Khonsu was seated on one.

"Did it go well?" He rose and came to Maïa.

"Yes, it went well." Words were hard to find; her eyes were still filled with the sight of Her Majesty's shining presence — her divine self. *From a prison mat to the throne room is a great journey for one morning,* she thought.

And she was not the only one making a great journey. Somewhere Uncle and Aunt traveled across the searing desert to their exile in an oasis. Aunt would complain about the day she had brought those two orphans into her house, but perhaps Uncle would be happy to be intact and not swimming with the crocodiles.

With one finger, Maïa touched the stiff Maat feather. She remembered how it had gleamed in the light of the throne room, how it had seemed hard and rigid. Even if she had not told all the truth about Uncle, justice had been done. But there was no joy in it. She would have to go to her friends and her mother's favorite goddess — Hathor — for that: for dancing, music, and beauty to take away the prison smell and to heal her wounds.

HISTORICAL NOTE

To be a scribe in the Eighteenth Dynasty — at the height of Egyptian civilization — in Thebes, the center of power and religion — was a fine position, indeed. A scribe could hold a position at court and travel on important missions, and people respected and asked his opinion.

Most often, scribes were boys who started school at the age of four, attending The House of Life at a nearby temple or in a teacher's house. But there is evidence of women who were scribes, and scholars think that Hatshepsut — one of the only female rulers in ancient Egypt — knew how to write.

Hatshepsut was the daughter of Tuthmosis I, a powerful king who ruled from c. 1504 to 1492 B.C.E., expanding the Egyptian empire with his large army. Following Egyptian custom, Hatshepsut wed her half-brother, Tuthmosis II, when she was about thirteen years of age and had at least one child by him. When her husband died, however, Hatshepsut ascended the throne. To consolidate her power and show her people that she was a legitimate ruler, Hatshepsut claimed she was chosen to rule by her father, Tuthmosis I, and that she was the divine child of the god Amun, himself.

It appears to have worked, and she presided over a time of extraordinary security and peace at home, ruling for nearly fifteen years. She mounted an expedition to the land of Punt (which may now be Somalia or southern Sudan) with five large boats, thirty rowers each. After two years they returned bearing exotic animals, spices, gold, and valuable incense trees that were planted at her mortuary temple at Deir el-Bahri.

She repaired and expanded many temples, including the one at Karnak, where she had installed two amazing 100-foot-tall obelisks of red granite, their tops sheathed in glittering gold. Shining as brightly as the sun and covered with hieroglyphs celebrating her accomplishments, these obelisks were a testimony to her glory and power.

Earlier historians thought that there was a battle of wills between her stepson, Tuthmosis III, who wished to rule alone, and Hatshepsut, who kept him from power. To support this theory, scholars pointed to the destruction of Hatshepsut's name and images in carvings and on statues. But recent historical opinion thinks that they reigned jointly for many years, with perhaps Hatshepsut controlling domestic affairs while her stepson took care of military matters.

To adequately cover Egyptian history would take far more space than is available in this note. But a brief summary of the glory of ancient Egypt — which stretched from about 3500 B.C.E. to 30 B.C.E. — would look at an astonishing array of accomplishments.

As early as 3500 B.C.E. we think Egyptians began writing, and they unified Upper and Lower Egypt; Upper actually being the southernmost part of Egypt, and Lower referring to the swampy delta country to the north, bordering on the Mediterranean.

The Old Kingdom, from c. 2705 to 2213 B.C.E., was a long and stable time that saw the development of a rule of law and the evolution of a rich and complex religion concerned with the afterlife and survival into the next world. The great pyramids were built during this period, but the era finally ended in turmoil, probably caused by weak flooding of the Nile and poor harvests.

In the later Middle Kingdom, c. 2061 to 1668 B.C.E., the Theban princes unified Egypt once again and presided over a time of increased agricultural production, a strong and consolidated military, fine art, and an expansion of trade. This period ended with the invasion of the Hykssos from the east, who ruled for many years. They brought the horse-drawn chariot, a stronger composite bow, and armor, all of which the Egyptians put to good use.

In the New Kingdom, the period of this book, the hated Hykssos invaders were conquered, and a time of peace and prosperity began. (How the Egyptians distrusted foreigners! And to die on foreign soil was worse than death itself.) Often, when you look at some of the most elegant and colorful tomb paintings, they are from this period, which lasted from c. 1550 to 1069 B.C.E.

One gets the sense that Egypt was a wonderful and joyful place to live. Although the life span was only about thirty-five years for a woman and thirty years for a man, they were a people who delighted in flowers, music, their religion, and the Nile, which brought life-giving floods each summer. It was a land of contrasts — red land (the desert) and black land (fertile fields), drought and plenty, extreme heat and a milder climate.

Egypt was probably one of the best places to be a woman in the ancient world. Women could own property and make their own wills. They could divorce their husbands and retain ownership of their property. They could bring cases to court and plead for justice. They could start their own businesses. Girls usually married between the ages of twelve and fourteen, and children were valued and a delight. Children, no matter their class, simply did not wear clothes in the early years, practical for such a hot climate.

And the emphasis on the afterlife and mummification? Some think it an obsession, but others — myself among them — think it is a sign of how much the Egyptians loved life. There, in the tomb (if you were well-to-do), your *ka* would live on in the beautiful paintings on the walls, eternally fed by images of bread and wine, geese, dates and figs, and cooled by the shaded ponds in their courtyards. There a blue lotus bloomed, its sweet scent perfuming a life that went on forever.

♦ Egyptians developed an early, accurate solar calendar of 365 days, with three ten-day weeks per month and five holidays at the new year. Although they measured hours by using water clocks in later dynasties, the smallest unit of time below that is simply a moment, an *at*.

♦ The Egyptians of a better class had bathrooms, stone-lined chambers with a drain in the middle. Using a paste made from water and natron, a kind of desert salt, many Egyptians bathed daily. A fastidious people, they may have used clay jugs with sand inside as a sort of early chamber pot.

♦ Hieroglyphs were created by the Egyptians probably before 3100 B.C.E. and could represent an idea, a word, or a sound. The signs carved on temples are more rigid, but in letters and documents, Egyptians developed a more slanted writing called *hieratic*. An even more informal and quicker form of handwriting called *demotic* was developed around 700 B.C.E.

- The Egyptians believed there was a weighing of the heart at the time of death, that it was set on a scale and balanced by a feather from Maat's headdress — representing truth and justice. If the heart did not balance, it was devoured by a monster, destroying the person forever.

- Egyptians loathed gray hair and baldness, using hair dyes to change hair color, or wigs to conceal baldness. Many shaved their heads and wore wigs anyway, finding it cooler in the heat and a better way to deal with head lice.

- Egyptians did not mint coins or use money to purchase items or to pay workers. Instead, they used barter at bustling markets; paid their workers in salt, fish, grains, and oil; or used a system of copper weights to determine the worth of an object.

ABOUT THE AUTHOR

Ann Turner is the author of acclaimed historical fiction, including the picture books *Katie's Trunk* and *Abe Lincoln Remembers*, as well as the historical novel *Grasshopper Summer* and, for the *Dear America* series, *The Girl Who Chased Away Sorrow* and *Love Thy Neighbor*.

She lives with her family in Williamsburg, Massachusetts.

ACKNOWLEDGMENTS

I would like to thank Shulamith Oppenheim for her help in researching this novel, and particularly Catharine Roehrig, Assistant Curator for the Egyptian Collection at the Metropolitan Museum of Art in New York City. I could not have written this book without her skilled and scholarly assistance. Any errors in research and writing are my own.

Atticus of Rome
30 B.C.

By Barry Denenberg

Pandora of Athens
399 B.C.

By Barry Denenberg